Mr Phillips

John Lanchester was born in Hamburg in 1962. He was brought up in the Far East and educated in England. He is a columnist for the *Daily Telegraph* and is on the editorial board of the *London Review of Books*. *The Debt to Pleasure*, his first novel, was translated into twenty languages, won the Whitbread First Novel Award, the Betty Trask Prize (for 'a first novel of a romantic or traditional nature'), the Hawthornden Prize (for a work of 'imaginative literature') and a Julia Child Award (for 'literary food writing').

by the same author

THE DEBT TO PLEASURE

JOHN LANCHESTER

Mr Phillips

Quality Paperbacks Direct
London

This edition published 2000
by QPD
By arrangement with Faber and Faber Limited

CN 4731

Typeset by Faber and Faber Ltd
Printed and bound in England by
Mackays of Chatham plc, Chatham Kent

For Miranda

A man left alone in the universe would have no rights whatsoever, but he would have obligations.

SIMONE WEIL, *The Need for Roots*

Mr Phillips

At night, Mr Phillips lies beside his wife and dreams about other women.

Not all of the dreams are about sex. Not all the women are real. There are dreams in which composite girls, no one he knows, look on while Mr Phillips goes about his dream-business of worrying about things, or looking for things, or feeling obscurely guilty about things. There is a dream he has been having since he was ten years old, in which he saves a whole group of strange women from certain disaster by diverting a runaway train or safely landing an aeroplane or encouraging them to hang on to the roof fittings on a tilting ship until just the right moment. He has even had a couple of dreams which involve him doing something vague but heroic in relation to the Channel Tunnel.

In the aftermath of these feats he is becomingly casual, almost dismissive. To camera crews and the world's press he explains that it is no big deal; but the women in the dream know that that isn't true.

Mr Phillips has anxious dreams about meeting the Queen and being awarded an honour, but not being able to remember what it is for. He has dreams about being told off by Mrs Thatcher. He has dreams about meeting his mother and not being sure whether they are in Australia (where, in real life, she lives, with Mr Phillips's sister), or London (where, in real life, he lives), or somewhere else. He once had a dream about Indira Gandhi. None of these dreams was about sex. He never told his wife about them. What good could come of it?

As for the sex dreams, he never told her about them, either. What good etc., only more so.

Mr Phillips grades them from one to ten. A one out of ten is quite mild. For instance, he often dreams about Christine Wilson, his next door neighbour but two when he was growing up in Wandsworth. At the age of twelve she was half a notch posher than most of the children in the street; she had brown hair worn in plaits and a naughty streak well hidden from grown-ups. Christine would often instigate uproar, though she was never blamed for causing it. Mr Phillips had gone from hardly noticing her to being horribly, drowningly in love with her in the course of a single Saturday. They had spent that day crawling around in the foundations of a new office building that was going up on land that had lain empty since a stray V2 had cleared it thirteen years before. They played hide-and-seek among the concrete mixers, ducking and scrabbling through partially built walls. When an adult shouted at them they ran home. As he lay in bed that night Mr Phillips found that he was very much in love.

In the dream, he and Christine are at school together, which in real life they never were. Mr Phillips sits next to her on a scratched wooden double desk which is covered in archaeo-

4

logical layers of graffiti. They are solving, under test conditions, a series of simple algebraic equations: $a + b = x$, if $a = 2$ and $x = 5$, what is b? He has an erection so strong that he is worried his flies are going to pop open. The end of the lesson is approaching and he is going to have to stand up and everyone is going to see his cock. The unfair thing is that he doesn't feel sexually aroused, he only has the erection because he's got caught up inside his underpants. In fact his penis is trapped outside the entrance to his knickers and is pinned vertically upwards. But no one will believe that. He wouldn't believe it in their shoes. In the dream he starts to blush, feeling the blood rush upwards and his face become lava-hot, electric-fire-hot. Then he wakes up. That is a one out of ten.

By three out of ten, the sex component is more definite. Mr Phillips is kissing his secretary Karen on the cheek while the telephone rings. He knows that he should pick up the receiver but Karen's eyes are closed and she looks so happy that he doesn't want to stop. He has such a good close-up view of the tiny hairs on the side of her neck that when he stops kissing her he says, 'You'll have to start shaving there soon.' She reaches down and puts a hand on his cock. Mr Monroe, the Aberdonian colleague with whom he shares an office and Karen's services, looks on approvingly. Then he wakes up.

A five out of ten sex dream might involve what used to be called 'heavy petting' or some form of explicit display. One of the most common of these dreams involves the television personality Clarissa Colingford. She has hair that is whitish blonde and what would once have been called 'a lovely figure' and eyes that are the same colour as the middle of a Mars bar. Mr Phillips is hiding in her cupboard, terrified and excited, as he watches her masturbate, covered only by a single thin cotton sheet. That is actually one of the most exciting of his dreams, but it only scores five since Mr Phillips's system is to grade the dreams not on how stimulating they are but on the explicitness of their sex content.

At seven out of ten the sex component is such that it becomes hard to meet the eye of the woman in the dream, the next time he meets her in real life. There is, for instance, something embarrassing or delirious about bumping into Janet – secretary to his boss Mr Mill, the incompetent head of the accountancy department – as she walks down the corridor with two plain digestive biscuits balanced on the saucer of a cup of tea, for all the world as if she had not, the night before, been eagerly responding to Mr Phillips's frightened but keen request to be sodomized with a nine-inch rubber penis.

It can't just be him, Mr Phillips feels. Office life is an erotic conspiracy. Everybody in offices thinks about sex all the time – that's exactly what they do. If the air at Wilkins and Co. were like one of those swimming pools which changes colour when someone pees in it, so that the air would be dyed blue whenever anyone looked on their colleagues with lust, or need, or at the very least sexual speculation, then the atmosphere would be as clogged and dense as a London pea-souper. Does he stalk rampant through the dreams of co-workers, a vivid principle of priapism, so that the working day carries the lurid after-tinge of the night before? Perhaps Karen herself has beguiled an idle moment by speculating as to what it would be like with Mr Phillips. After all, she's only human. People fall in love with their secretaries all the time, and vice versa – not least because most men are at their most attractive when at work, their attention directed outside themselves, with chores to perform and decisions to make, all unlike the sulking, shifty tyrants of the domestic stage, wanting everything their own way and locked in a battle to the death to get it.

It goes without saying that people use offices for sex all the time, too. It's a rare photocopier that hasn't been used to take a picture of somebody's bum. It's a very unusual desk that has never had people fucking on it. In an important sense, all this is what offices are for. Mr Phillips has even done it on a desk himself once, when he was working at Grimshaw's, his first employer. His girlfriend Sharon Mitchell came to the office late to collect him on the way to a film, a Western with James Stewart in it. This was in the days before security guards and after-hours subcontracted office cleaners. They had done it on Mr Phillips's very own desk, indeed on his very own ink blotter. Sharon was the first girl Mr Phillips did it with who was on the pill; she chucked him for a musician. A sixties memory.

One thing that all the dreams have in common is that Mr Phillips never actually manages to have sex in them. Even in the ten out of ten dreams, Mr Phillips never gets it wet. He looks and sees and feels and kisses, he plots and schemes and gets women to agree to have sex with him, and in some versions they even pursue him to ask for it ('begging for it', 'gagging for it') but he never, in the dreams, actually puts his penis inside another person, not even in the homosexual dreams which come along every now and then, with their own agenda, as if trying to make a point.

This morning, Mr Phillips has just woken from a seven out of ten dream in which he was trying to arrange to have sex with Miss Pettifer, his younger son Thomas's form teacher at St Francis Xavier's. She is in her early fifties and therefore around the same age as Mr Phillips. In real life, he hasn't been conscious of being even vaguely attracted to her – but when he wakes after the dream, he realizes that isn't the whole story. The fact that she is, say, twenty pounds overweight, he feels in part of himself as a liberation, as if, in throwing off one set of worries about being sensible and watching your weight, other worries might be thrown off too, so that her half-double chin and wildly blossoming hips, all the more visible because her clothes are a third of a size too small, hold a promise: with me, you can do *anything you want*.

This isn't the first time he has dreamt about Miss Pettifer. The last time it happened he made an effort to talk to her at the next PTA meeting, as a way of getting the dream out of his system. When they shook hands, in the tobacco-stained staff room which smelt of instant coffee, he had the feeling that there was something in her eyes beyond the usual struggle to remember who this particular parent was. Perhaps she was

8

aware that she had spent at least part of one night trying to clear a space among the desks or find a cupboard where he could fuck her standing up among brooms and brushes and ironing boards. (That is a detail from the dream that had to be wrong – why would the school have ironing boards in the cupboard?) But they were constantly interrupted: people came in and out, children playing cricket in the corridors kept bursting in to ask Mr Phillips if he would be their umpire, and once Martin, Mr Phillips's elder son, came knocking on the door of the cubicle in the bathroom just as Miss Pettifer had undone Mr Phillips's fly and extracted his penis.

As Mr Phillips begins to wake up, by instalments, reality gradually coalesces around him in the form of his bedroom, his house, his sheets, which are wedding presents still surviving nicely more than two decades after the event, the photographs of his sons in a silver frame on top of the dressing table, and his wife, behind whom he is curled, underneath whose buttocks his erection, harder than those he now usually comes up with, is squeezed. Over her back and shoulder Mr Phillips can see the bits and pieces on their shared bedside table:

– a lamp, an impulse purchase of Mrs Phillips's, slightly too low to cast a valuable reading light;

– a glass of water, undrunk, which by morning would always have undergone a change in taste and become oddly flat;

– an alarm clock in the shape of an owl, a present from Thomas, with luminous hands, and ears which have to be wound to make the clock go; Mr Phillips can never remember whether the left ear wound the clock and the right the alarm or vice versa;

– his reading glasses, black-framed and substantial, like the ones Michael Caine wore as secret agent Harry Palmer in *The Ipcress File*;

– a cloth doily, fringed and trimmed with lace, given them by

– a pupil of Mrs Phillips's as a Christmas present, which was initially supposed to have been given away or thrown out but gradually evolved into a stable member of the domestic fittings (since it did, in the final analysis, keep drink-rings off the furniture);

– a copy of Mrs Phillips's current reading: *The Choir* by Joanna Trollope;

– a copy of one of Tom's football magazines, which Mr Phillips had picked up by mistake, thinking it was one of his *Economist*s;

– a copy of Bobby Moore's autobiography; Mr Phillips tends to read only autobiographies and memoirs, on the grounds that there is something comforting about them, perhaps to do with the fact that the hero never dies at the end;

– a two-thirds full box of tissues.

But more important than any of these is the feel of Mrs Phillips. They fit so well together when they are asleep. Lying there, Mr Phillips can be sure that nothing else in the day will be as good as lying curling around his wife, half-asleep in the gap between being half-woken by aeroplanes going in to land at Heathrow and the detonation of the alarm clock. Sleep and dreams and bed are close to an infantile state for Mr Phillips. That's no criticism; that's the way he likes them. If he and Mrs Phillips had been cocooned in the womb together, he thinks they would have got along fine. Though in the womb he would have missed the smell of her, of which again he was never as acutely aware as he is now, her skin smelling of milk and sometimes cinnamon, her hair of leaves or sometimes, not unpleasantly, of London, a smell like distant gun smoke (any stronger than that and she would have washed it), or of the floral aftermath of her previous day's toilette, and of sweat, metallic and musky, perhaps even of the farts which might have been democratically intermingling under the duvet, with an occasional whiff of authentic cunt-smell wafting up as she shifts beside him. Sometimes, after she used spermicide, the interaction of nonoxyl-9 and her body heat would by the next morning have magically produced the aroma of toasted almonds.

It is Mr Phillips's usual practice, when he wakes up, to think about something semi-worrying, like his tax return or Tom's proposal to 'borrow' the house for a party, as a way of getting himself warmed up for the day. One reliable source of worry and irritation is the very thing that has woken him up, the sound of aeroplanes going overhead to land at Heathrow. Already today they are roaring over at ninety-second intervals. This morning, as on most mornings, the planes would have begun passing overhead at a little bit after four a.m. At first they would be irregular, a plane every few minutes or so, but now, by half past six, they have settled down to a steady rhythm. Some mornings Mr Phillips sleeps all the way through, and doesn't wake until his alarm clock gets him up at half past seven. Other mornings the very first plane would sound as if it were landing, not at Heathrow a dozen miles away, but in the front garden, and Mr Phillips would be woken as efficiently and crudely as if someone had come into the room and shaken him. Then he would stay awake, shifting and twitching and listening to the planes, for three hours, only to fall asleep two minutes before it was time to get up. Did the people on board the planes ever give any thought to the thousands of would-be sleepers that they were waking up?

Mr Phillips has a cross between a story and a day-dream which he tells himself about the planes:

Minutes of the Three-Monthly Meeting of the Wellesley Crescent Neighbourhood Watch Association

1) Apologies for absence

2) Reading minutes of last meeting

3) Further business

PRESENT: *Mr Tomkins (chair), Mr Davis-Gribben, Mr Phillips, Mr Palmer (secretary), Mr Morris, Miss Griffin, Mr Cartwright, Mr and Mrs Wu*

1) Apologies for absence.
Mr Cott called from a payphone at St George's Hospital to say that he could not come because they had not finished with him yet. There were no other apologies for absence.

2) The minutes of the last meeting were read and agreed.

3) Further business.

a) Mr Davis-Gribben reported that there had been two incidents of car crime in the Crescent. Mrs Palmer had her car tax disc stolen, though she says herself it was partly her fault because she did not check that the passenger door was locked because her Renault does not have central locking which is what she was used to on her old Honda. But they did not try to take her radio which she was pleased about.

A left-hand drive camper van with German number plates that had been parked in the Crescent had its offside front window broken.

b) Mr Tomkins reported that the mystery of the unidentified dog that had been seen wandering up and down the Crescent for a fortnight towards the end of June, about which Police Constable Carson had been called, had been solved. The dog, who was called Kevin, belonged to a Mr and Mrs Hildon from Gallipoli Row, near the train station. Mr and Mrs Hildon's son Rory had returned from college for his summer holidays having become a vegetarian and he had insisted that the rest of the household become vegetarians too. This Mr and Mrs Hildon had been willing to do because otherwise Rory would move out for the whole of the holidays and they see little enough of him as it is, but the special vegetarian dog food had been too much for Kevin and he had run away. He had been found because Mrs Palmer saw a notice in the big post office beside the train station where she had gone to pick up an application form for a new car tax registration thingy when the first one was stolen. The Hildons had been very pleased to be reunited with Kevin and Rory had then and there sat down and had a bacon sandwich.

c) The question of graffiti on the sign for Wilmington Park was raised and it was agreed that Mr Tomkins would write a letter to the council on behalf of the Wellesley Crescent Neighbourhood Watch, asking that something be done.

d) Mr Davis-Gribben brought up the issue of the noise from the aircraft passing overhead in the small hours of the morning to land at Heathrow. He said that he had written to the British Airports Authority and to the local MP and to the council and had been fobbed off with standard replies. He said that everyone he knew felt at the end of their tether about the noise and that he hadn't had a night's sleep in months, and although it was not an expression he often used, he agreed with a minicab driver he had spoken to the other day who said that the noise was doing his head in. He asked if anyone had any suggestions for further action.

Mr Cartwright said that his brother who was in the Army had been to stay and had been woken up by the noise every night for a week. His brother had then suggested that they should get hold of a ground to air missile and shoot an aeroplane down. He said that air traffic into Heathrow would drop away dramatically afterwards. Mr Cartwright said that he had been looking into the possibility of acquiring a ground to air missile, purely from the feasibility point of view, and that the most promising source appeared to be the Stinger missiles which the CIA had given to the Mujahedeen guerrillas fighting the Soviet-backed regime in Afghanistan during the 1980s. He said that the CIA had supplied a thousand missiles, of which about 700 had been used and that they had shot down over 500 Soviet planes and helicopters, which was an impressive strike rate.

The CIA had tried to buy back the missiles at a rate of US$1 million each but many of them were still in the hands of the guerrillas.

Mr Phillips reminded other members that the budget for Wellesley Crescent Neighbourhood Watch for the current year was £47, most of which went on photocopying and biscuits.

Mr Cartwright conceded the point but said that the Mujahedeen might be willing to give them a missile once they explained what it was for. He added that the guerrillas could be shown a map of Wilmington Park, just at the end of the road and always deserted at night, and they would see that it was an ideal point from which to launch a Stinger missile at a plane flying only a couple of hundred feet overhead.

Mr Davis-Gribben wondered who would go and get the missile and how it would be brought back.

Mr Cartwright said that he would go and get the missile. His first wife, with whom he was still on good terms, was a Mrs Khan whose family were from Lahore. He could go and visit them before making a side trip to Afghanistan. He said that he had consulted a map and that it was not far. He would smuggle the missile over the border into Turkey where it would be collected by his cousin Roger, a long-distance lorry driver who often did the Ankara route.

Mr Tomkins wondered what would happen if the plane were shot down and it landed somewhere inside the borough of Wandsworth. If there were a disaster in the borough would it not place enormous financial strain on local services and result in much higher council tax bills?

Mr Phillips said that to the best of his knowledge the cost of these *sorts of disaster was borne by central government. He wondered if the Wellesley Crescent Neighbourhood Watch ought to send a warning as to the action they intended to take, so that it was correctly interpreted as a protest against the aircraft noise and not claimed for their own handiwork by unscrupulous terrorists? Mr Cartwright agreed but Mr Davis-Gribben and Mr Morris did not. Mrs Wu pointed out that there was no hurry to resolve this point.*

Mrs Phillips shifts in bed and Mr Phillips holds still so as not to wake her. The bed this morning smells warm and slightly sweaty, though not of almonds. That smell is much, much less common than it had once been. These days there is probably no need for the spermicide, Mr Phillips thinks, given that he is fifty and Mrs Phillips is . . . forty-six. (When he thinks of his wife's age he always has a split-second flash of panic while he checks the date. Birthday, 14 October 1948; today's date, 31 July 1995 – phew. Two months plus still to go. And nearly six months till the wedding anniversary, 14 January. Mr Phillips has a recurring fear that one day he will remember one of these dates only to find that it is too late, he has already forgotten it, notwithstanding its red-inked presence in the diary and in the reliable memory of Karen, and he will be involved in an orgy of self-abasement and apology and also the nagging doubt about why he had forgotten – was the marriage running out of steam, or was his memory fading, or both? Marriage being, like the religion Mr Phillips gave up long ago, a matter of both faith and works, of sustained will-to-belief and routine observances, both being necessary and neither sufficient.)

One day the almond smell will become a thing of the past, gone for ever. Is anyone to blame, wonders Mr Phillips, or is this just what happens? He has discovered that there is a great secret about sex, a secret that far exceeds the other secrets that surrounded it when he was looking forward to it in youth – when sex was a country of possibility, the territory of films and pop music, the most forbidden, most exciting thing in the world. Sex itself was a secret into which you were initiated once and for all; everything about it was to do with secrets, some of which weren't true ('a girl can't get pregnant unless she comes', 'if you wank too much you'll go blind') and some of which, it turned out, were true (like the fact that it was the best thing in the world). But all those secrets are as nothing compared to the real secret, the truth no one wants to tell you and which even adults don't discuss or admit, and which, like all important secrets, is surprising and radical and obvious: it is that *no one ever does it*. This isn't strictly true, of course: some people do do it – but as a maxim, the idea that *no one ever does it* is certainly much, much more true than the opposite claim, that *everyone does it all the time*. No one Mr Phillips knows ever does it, anyway; not his horrible immediate boss Mr Mill or his horrible ultimate boss Mr Wilkins, not his colleagues, Aberdonian Mr Monroe or young Mr Abbot or drunk Mr Collins or bald Mr Austen; not his neighbours, the Cartwrights on the left (who instead have noisy, drunken bi-monthly Friday or Saturday night arguments) and the Cotts on the right (who are, however, in their seventies, so their obviously-not-doing-it-ness is both taken for granted and gratefully received, and you don't even have to think about them doing it), certainly not the Davis-Gribbens's opposite, who not only don't now do it but to judge by their childlessness have perhaps never done it, not even once, experimentally or to get it over with or by mistake. What is that brutal old wives' adage? If you put a penny in a jar for every time you did it during the first year of being married, then took a penny out for every time you did it thereafter, the jar would never become empty. Cruel but fair, thinks Mr Phillips. The accountant in him likes the fact that the size of the jar doesn't have to be specified.

So how often do we do it, he wonders; seriously, how often? It's hard to get an exact figure because everything human tends to go in clumps. It's like football, where teams go from a losing run to a winning run and you find that one minute Crystal Palace (Mr Phillips's team) have gone six games without a win and the next they've gone five without conceding a goal and the next they haven't been beaten at home since February. Everything is like that. They haven't done it since the day that Thomas fell off his mountain bike and broke his arm, which is five and a bit weeks ago. Mr Phillips got the call to go and collect him from Casualty on a Saturday afternoon – a flashback to the boys' childhoods, when it seemed that he spent half his time ferrying them back and forth to hospital with bone-breaks and sudden allergies, and the time Martin had bitten the thermometer in half and the nurse very surprisingly had said it was nothing really to worry about. Perhaps there was some complicated flashback aspect to their doing it that night? But they had also done it three days before that, after drinking a bottle of champagne which one of Mrs Phillips's pupils had given her to celebrate passing Grade Eight piano. So on the basis of that week's statistical blip they do it twice a week, which is almost the national average, though Mr Phillips is professionally suspicious of that figure.

He had once mentioned these doubts to Mr Monroe.

'I have never been at all confident of the numbers which tend to be mentioned,' Mr Monroe had said. He is a well organized former pipe-smoker with a dry, tight, friendly voice. He likes to talk, not in a running commentary on the day's events, as some office-sharers in Mr Phillips's experience preferred to do, but in chunks, as if he had settled down with his pipe. 'The unreliability of all self-reporting statistics is something which need only be mentioned to be seen as decisive. In this particular case, when you bear in mind the number of single people, children, grandmothers, widows, priests and nuns and incarcerated felons, Highlanders in their distant crofts, the impotent, not forgetting the irreparably hideous, the proposed national average of twice or twice and a half or even three times a week seems to me to be a lubricious fantasy.'

'To make up the numbers you'd have to have some people somewhere doing it fifty times a day,' said Mr Phillips. He and Mrs Phillips, realistically, did it probably once a month, a level to which they had dropped gradually but with a couple of marked dips when Martin and Tom were born. They had been out of their minds with fatigue, opportunities seemed non-existent, and suddenly they were that thing which when you

21

were younger you never imagined possible: *too tired for sex.*

In fact, they had hardly been doing it at all when Mrs Phillips conceived Thomas, nine years younger than Martin – once a fortnight perhaps (twenty-six times a year, therefore a 26 in 365 chance of doing it on any given day). Mr Phillips remembers the sex well, after a Christmas party at the Walters's – he being a colleague who subsequently transferred to Cardiff and was never heard of again. Mr Phillips had only just been sober enough to maintain a viable erection, but had been drunk enough to be very keen on the idea of sex, an excitement partly derived from the sight of other men's wives, especially Mrs Walters, who wore a backless dress that showed off bony shoulders and a liverous freckly back and was ugly/sexy in the same way Miss Pettifer had been in last night's dream. Her face seemed to have been put together absent-mindedly – nose just too high, or mouth too low, bunched male-looking lips, thick eyebrows, somehow monkey-like. She had stood so close, while talking to Mr Phillips in the party crush on the Walters's ludicrous jungle-dense fitted carpet, that he could feel the warmth rising off her body; if he had been someone else he might have made a pass. Instead – Thomas, now asleep in his cave-like bedroom.

Mr Phillips had mentioned the figure of once a month to Mr Monroe, and they had agreed to treat this purely hypothetical example to some number-crunching.

'Once a month is twelve times a year,' said Monroe, tapping at his Psion organiser. 'Twelve divided by 365 multiplied by

100 gives a 3.28767 per cent chance of our hypothetical couple, let's call them our virtual couple, having sex on any given day, or to put it another way, on the same given day there is a 96.71233 per cent probability of their not having sex.'

'Not that people always do it the same amount,' said Mr Phillips. 'It sort of comes and goes.'

'Aye, to be completely accurate you would have to build in the way the probability changes over time, and allow for the fact that the day after doing it the probability of doing it again will be very low, 1 per cent or less, gradually rising over time to a few weeks later when it might almost become more likely than not, say 50.01 per cent, or if your chappie spends three months in Antarctica or in prison or something, a well-nigh racing certainty.'

At the moment, the closest to a sure thing in Mr Phillips's sex life is the fact that they almost always have sex, or make love, or fuck, or – to use the phrase Mr Phillips uses in his innermost being, the basic, fundamental plumb level of his attitude to sex – 'do it' after going to see a film. Any film, not just sexy ones. Afterwards, Mrs Phillips is demonstrably keener on the idea and Mr Phillips himself is readier for it, as if psychic sap had irresistibly risen while he was sitting peering forwards in the crowded dark. Perhaps it is nothing more than the body heat of strangers, or the tacit admission of a universal appetite for voyeurism; in Mr Phillips's view, no one who has ever been to a film can claim that he doesn't like to watch. Or perhaps that the faces on screen were magnified and close, all their grain visible, in the way that only faces during sex are close; the only time we ever see each other in such detail and with such urgency. (In Mr Phillips's opinion, the sexiest film ever made was *The Railway Children*, though he knows you aren't supposed to say that.) But they only went three or four times a year. Videos didn't have the same effect. For a moment Mr Phillips wonders what happened when people became film critics. Perhaps they were the people who bumped up the averages.

However, even allowing for the films, Mr Phillips is still left with an average daily probability of 96.7 per cent against having sex. As an accountant, he has to admit that is a pretty grim figure. Was it for this, Mr Phillips wonders, as he rolls on his back and looks up at the ceiling – a Dulux white stained cream-coloured by the sun coming in through the yellow curtains – Mrs Phillips, always a more determined sleeper than he, still far gone by his side – was it for this that he, stranded on the cliff edge of pubescence, had looked forward to adulthood as a limitless ocean of sex? Those years when every allusion to sex, even words like 'thing' or 'it' or even, God help him, 'dog' (because the opposite of 'cat', which was cognate with 'pussy'), could ensure an instant hard-squeezed snigger? Those years of masturbating, of doing it, not to be confused with Doing It, for the years before he got to Do It for real for the first time with Maureen, his first girlfriend at college?

As for that almond smell, a couple using the cap and having sex a normal amount, whatever that meant, have a 94 per cent chance of not making a baby by the end of a given year. If he and Mrs Phillips did it once a month and the supposed average was ten times a month (2.5 times a week times four weeks), notwithstanding Mr Monroe's justified scepticism about that figure, then they did it a tenth of the average. Their ages made it even less likely, say a tenth as likely as when they were fully fertile. So their chance of conception was 10 per cent of 6 per cent, i.e. 0.6 per cent, i.e. not very high. When you took into account the fact of their age, the cap seems not so much a necessity as a votary tribute to the biological forces that are wavering and flickering inside them like broken pilot lights. In any case, for all these reasons, that almond smell is a lot more rare than it used to be.

At about seven o'clock, Mr Phillips hears the dustbin lorry
turn into the far end of the street. The dustmen call to each
other, shout, bang bins, swear, make noises that are associated with the effort of heaving bags up on to the back of the
cart, all the sounds which are always different but always
the same. The lorry is part of its being Monday, a process
which started last thing at night on Sunday with remembering to put out the rubbish – an action which is more complicated than it once was, since the council now recycles waste,
and there are different coloured plastic bags and different
weekly schedules for paper and plastics and bottles. Cardboard, however, you still have either to put in with the normal rubbish or take up to the council tip by the dog track,
which Mr and Mrs Phillips have formally decided, after
doing it what felt like a million times, they can no longer be
bothered to do.

The Monday feeling is under normal circumstances a fairly
pleasant one, given the pressures exerted by the structure of
the standard week: Mr Phillips feels that if he were blind-
folded, disoriented, whirled round and round, given mind-
altering drugs, deprived of external stimuli and calendars, but
was still allowed to keep his mood, he would be able to work

out what day of the week it was. Monday, along with its awful back-to-workness, contains a tinge of relief, of the bracing moment after the plunge into the icy pool when we realize the worst of the shock is over. Tuesdays are his least favourite weekday, since they lack the get-on-with-it feeling of Mondays, and at the same time the next weekend is still an impossible way off, and since, in addition, Mr Phillips was once told by a waiter in a Greek restaurant that Tuesdays are unlucky. Wednesdays still have the ghostly presence of school half-days benignly hanging over them. Thursdays are potentially heavy going, but do at least begin the ascent of good spirits that climb further through Fridays, about which Mr Phillips feels the same way as everybody else – Thank God It's Friday, Piss Off Early Tomorrow's Saturday – and Saturday is simply and gloriously Saturday, also much the most likely night of the week on which to have the monthly fuck. Sunday has its particular stalled feeling, which Mr Phillips is surprised to find has survived the instigation of Sunday trading and the arrival of Sunday football, and still clings to the day, an immovable, heavy, gravitational tug of depressive Sundayness. You could feel the week coming, and it felt bad.

As the dustbin lorry rumbles around the corner at the end of Wellesley Crescent, Mrs Phillips stirs but does not wake. Mr Phillips opens his eyes and decides he is now officially awake. He gets out of bed and pads to the bathroom in his striped pyjamas. When he gets to the mirror he sees that the open button of the jacket discloses a mass of grey and white curling chest hair, two shades further gone than what remains of the hair on his head.

Now, at fifty, Mr Phillips finds that his body – which has served him very well in some respects, only causing him to miss three days of work in his entire adult life – is, if not revolting, then at least acting like a rebellious province, tired of being ignored by central authority. In one absolutely central and literal sense he is ten years old – everything to do with feeling, with emotion, with excitement, with girls, with not being able to stop himself; and in another absolutely central way he feels he is nineteen – everything to do with the body, with its transparency to his will: if he wants to walk across London for a bet, or swim across the Thames at the turn of the tide, or beat up someone who scratches his car with a manly, straightforward right hook. But he only has to look in the mirror, or simply look down, to see his grey hair, his breasts, his sheer fleshiness, especially its outward-sloping, rounded, sagging silhouette. His body isn't his body, except of course that it is. His crazy religious education teacher at school, Mr Erith, had once embarked on a famous rant about St Augustine's claim that the penis was proof of original sin because it was resistant to the will and so it was a constant reminder of our disobedience, our fallen state. To Mr Phillips it is much too easy, just blaming his cock. It goes so much further than that. Mr Phillips's whole body, more or less, is resistant to the will, when it comes to walking up a flight of stairs without getting puffed, or chopping firewood without slipping a disc when they rented a cottage in the country, or even just looking in the mirror and not seeing something which makes him feel queasy.

On the way back from peeing and brushing his teeth, Mr Phillips pauses outside the door of Tom's bedroom. An apparently genuine NO ENTRY sign hangs there. It has taken considerable forbearance on Mr and Mrs Phillips's part to avoid asking where the sign came from, since that would either produce a heated denial of any illegality (if it had been, as Mr Phillips suspected, stolen) or a pained but triumphantly self-righteous brandishing of a receipt from, say, a novelty shop (which is what Mrs Phillips thought: 'It looks far too new.') It's hard not to see your own flaws in your children, thinks Mr Phillips. Thomas is never angrier than when he is in the wrong, and never more irritating than when he is in the right. Mr Phillips has no difficulty in recognizing that. Martin, on the other hand, has the ability to be good-naturedly and fixedly in the wrong – it doesn't seem to bother him. Mr Phillips first noticed this ability when his son was ten and broke a clock in the sitting room by hitting it with a tennis racket, observed by Mrs Phillips's mother, who was baby-sitting one year old Tom upstairs and who, unbeknown to Martin, had come down to make a cup of tea. Martin denied the accident, or crime, with total vehemence, despite the fact that it had been witnessed, until he all of a sudden ceased to deny it, blushing and smiling and apologizing all at once. Mr Phillips saw that although his son minded being in the wrong to some extent, he didn't really mind it the way most of us do – at which Mr Phillips felt a pang of fear and wonder at his offspring's alien life, either unprotected or doubly protected by this enviable and mysterious heedlessness.

There is no noise whatsoever from Tom's room. He is out cold, as usual; Tom sleeps an astonishing, inexplicable amount. But Mr Phillips can remember that he had wanted to sleep all the time at that age too, except that his father wouldn't let him. The only domestic task that Michael Phillips ever performed was bringing his son a cup of tea on weekend and holiday mornings – as if in preparation for an adulthood of abrupt awakenings and departures, in which you were in need of constant vigilance. He saw adult life as a contest, a decathlon without the lightheartedness or the fellow-feeling between contestants.

Mr Phillips doesn't agree; he thinks that his son needs all the sleep he can get. In his view, teenagers sleep so much because they are preparing for the insomniac and sleep-shortened times ahead: the knackering first few years of working and socializing (Mr Phillips was exhausted for the first two years of full employment at Grimshaw's, often falling asleep on the train home); the unimaginable exhaustion of young parenthood, with its broken nights, incessant physical and emotional labour, and the trench warfare of raising small children; the different fatigue of later adulthood, that of sheer accumulated livedness, the sense that nothing again would ever be new or surprising, that vital reserves of energy and luck had been critically and irreversibly depleted. As you grow older, sleep somehow becomes thinner, as if the fabric of unconsciousness itself is becoming stretched and febrile; you don't go down as far or for as long; as if the permanent period of rest in the rapidly approaching future is already exerting an effect, in the way that one recovers reserves of energy as soon as the end of a boring film or dinner party finally heaves into sight. Sleep is a bank account that you put capital in when you are young and draw on as you get older; and then you run out of capital and die.

Mr Phillips puts his ear against the door of his son's room and listens for a moment to the silence. Left to his own devices, Tom will never come downstairs before midday, and when he does so will wordlessly take a bowl of cornflakes and a cup of Nescafé from the kitchen to flop down in front of the television. If he is up before noon on Saturday he will turn on a pop music programme, which Mr Phillips secretly likes to watch, because the videos often have erotic content in the form of writhing girls. I know what they're doing but I don't understand why they're trying to do it standing up, as the old buffers used once to say. He can however tell that his presence has a suffocating effect on Tom. Perhaps his son's motive for watching the programme is sufficiently close to his own to make the moment embarrassingly intimate; or perhaps watching anything to do with sex in the company of our parents is to some extent the same as watching our parents have sex. Last Saturday, two days before, Mr Phillips went downstairs to find

31

Tom watching a video which, to the sound of the usual arrhythmical crashing and wailing, consisted of nothing more than a girl's beautiful tea-coloured midriff, her navel pierced with a single thin band of gold, wiggling from side to side, up and down, a glimpse of low-slung skirt intermittently visible at the bottom of the shot, which was otherwise without distractions. Images which in Mr Phillips's youth would have been considered pornographic are now everywhere, an accepted visual language; and all to the good, thinks Mr Phillips. Well done! On the back cover of the current issue of *Vogue*, for instance, an indulgence Mrs Phillips allows herself every few months, is a beautifully lavish black and white photograph of a woman's bottom – and a very small bottle of perfume. Well done! Mr Phillips, standing, and Tom, lying, had watched the girl's wiggling in embarrassed but rapt silence for ninety seconds until Mr Phillips had said:

'That must hurt.' – an attempted reference to the navel ring. Mr Phillips could hear the middle-agedness in his voice and hated it. Tom hadn't even looked up at him, and he left the room.

Sometimes an image from a telly programme, or from a woman seen in the street, or even a sexy memory that just popped up for no reason, will lodge in Mr Phillips's mind like a splinter under a fingernail and stay there for weeks, so that he finds himself replaying it over and over again (the expression in the eyes of Sharon Mitchell, blank with lust, as she turned her head to look at him as he slid his cock into her from behind on her parents' downstairs divan: a thirty year old memory that one day, as he was masturbating in the bath, popped up in front of his imagination like a projected slide). At the moment the image tormenting him is of Clarissa Colingford, surely not her real name, whom Mr Phillips had first seen on some show in which celebrities made fools of themselves for charity. She had been doing the locomotion, and something about the way she did it, mechanically precise in her choo-chooing motion, embarrassed but also abandoned, smiling and blushing at the same time, had snagged at Mr Phillips, so that he couldn't stop thinking about her. It was something to do with the hinterland of life you could guess in her, the background life of getting out of bed in the morning, checking her answering machine messages, swearing when she stubbed her toe, popping out for cat food and dental floss, putting bank statements in the bin without opening them – you could picture her doing all these things in the same busy, preoccupied, sexily absent-minded way. Mr Phillips could tell they would like each other if they met. She was the sort of person you could tell at say a fourth meeting that you'd had a dream about them, or even, conceivably, if you really *were* getting on, that you'd had a crush on them for ages. Mr Phillips has to admit that he would be capable of making a fool of himself for Clarissa Colingford. And as chance would have it, just as Mr Phillips was becoming obsessed with her, so everyone else seemed to be too. She had caught the public imagination and suddenly there were appearances on panel games and tabloid stories about boyfriend trouble. She was famous in that pure, almost abstract, modern way, a celebrity. If you stopped someone in the street and asked if they had heard of Clarissa Colingford the answer would probably be Yes. If you asked what it was she was best known for, there would probably be a sticky pause. But the truth was, who needed to be known for anything when they could have Clarissa's pure, blonde, above-it-all innocent sexiness?

On mornings when he leaves the house to go to work, Mr Phillips comes out of the front door and stops for a moment while he runs his eye over the trellis beside the bay window. Mrs Phillips's climbers are struggling again. While he does this he surreptitiously checks the street for the presence of neighbours. Even though he basically gets on with most of them, thanks in no small part to the Wellesley Crescent Neighbourhood Watch Association, Mr Phillips nonetheless feels a small but vivid dislike of bumping into them at this point in the day, as they head off to work with closed, practical faces. The worst of them is the extraordinarily nosy Mr Palmer at number 42, known to the Phillips family as Norman the Noxious Neighbour. Mr Phillips's mood lifts slightly whenever he sees that the coast is clear. Today there is no Norman but he does have to walk past Mr Morris at number 32, five doors down, as he stands in a track suit beside the open door of his big car.

'Morning,' says Mr Phillips.

'Morning,' says, or rather grunts, Mr Morris – evidently this isn't his favourite ritual either. And it is a nice enough morning, for London anyway, already warm, the blue sky reasonably visible between chunky but fast moving, whiter-than-usual clouds.

The houses in the Crescent are low-squatting semi-detached Edwardian villas – a word which always gives Mr Phillips a mental glimpse of people in togas on the set of *Up Pompeii*. They look more cramped than they are, with decent space at the back and sometimes an attic too, as well as three upstairs bedrooms. If houses were faces the street would be a row of well-fed Tories, golfers, Gilbert and Sullivan enthusiasts. Now that Martin has left home their house has gone from near population overload to being eerily roomy, and Mr Phillips has taken over the loft (formerly Martin's lair) as a study or den. From it he looks out over neighbours' gardens and the roofscape towards the tower block about half a mile away. In his den he mostly studies second-hand car prices or reads one of his autobiographies.

At the end of the road Mr Phillips turns left again and heads down Middleton Way, today as on every work day. This street is used as a cut-through by cars trying to defeat the one-way system, even though so many drivers know the route that it's just as clogged and congested as the official route – a typical London event, in a city where knowing the wrinkles and shortcuts only helps as long as not enough others know them too. Today the cars in the cut-through sit fuming and revving in the July warmth, the air already close and polluted. Mr Phillips watches the inhabitant of a dark blue L-reg Vauxhall Astra, a thirtyish man with a suit jacket hung in his off-side rear window, pick his nose, consider the product of his excavation and then, with a decisive gourmandly air, eat it. Three cars in front, a woman in a VW Passat is leaning over and using the rear-view mirror to check between her front teeth.

Mr Phillips turns into Kestrel Lane opposite the chemist, whose window displays are one of the most reliable indicators of the changing seasons. Today it's hay fever medicine, which is advertised by a huge, transparent three-dimensional model of a head with the nose and the sinuses blocked with red tubular fillings to indicate mucus. Bye bye hay fever, bye bye drowsiness, says the poster. When Mr Phillips took his A-levels – 1963, a decade after the end of rationing, an event he can still remember – the invigilator, a supply teacher he had never set eyes on before, had been suffering from the worst case of hay fever he had ever seen, his eyes bloodshot and liquid, nose running, breathing heavily through his mouth. They had all thought that was hilarious. Hay fever was rarer then than now; the whole city has allergies, it's the nitric oxide. It beats up your immune system so the other stuff gets through to you more easily. Even Mr Phillips's doctor came down with asthma, at the age of forty-five.

A white man with dreadlocks comes out of the chemists and is greeted by his eager dog, who is wearing a collar made out of a red ribbon.

Pedestrians stream past in every direction, most of them dressed for the working day, most of them in a hurry.

Mr Phillips stops in front of the travel agent, two doors down. There are posters in the window of happy people in places with good weather. A woman of about twenty-five watches her husband batting a large beach ball into the air while two small sandy children tug at his legs. In the middle distance of another photograph, a man learns to windsurf. Child-free couples walk on beaches in front of a cinema sunset. Standing and looking at the pictures, Mr Phillips has a vision of himself beside a swimming pool somewhere hot. At his right side, a cold drink beaded with sweat and icy to the touch. At his left, Karen the secretary, face down, in a leopard print bikini, tiny volcanic irregularities of smoochable cellulite crawling under her bikini bottoms, a stray brown pubic hair visible to the truly attentive eye, her back also beaded with sweat, shiny with suntan oil, hot to the touch. On his stomach, which is flatter than in real life, Mr Phillips balances a copy of the *Daily Mail*, where he is reading about Europe's triumph over America in the Ryder Cup, or England's over Australia in the Ashes, or studying a business story about how some company in which he just happens to have bought lots of shares has surged 1000 per cent upwards in a week, or looking at the fashion pages and picking out a pink frock with a slashed shoulder whose scooped ovoid neckline would suit Karen only too well. A list of prices for flights hangs beside one for all-in holiday packages:

Malaga £179 for 2 weeks *Morocco £219 return*
San Francisco £239 return *Costa Rica £299 return*
Faro £85 return *New York £190 return*
Alicante £84 return *Paris city break from £109 room*
Atlanta £229 return *£15 p.p.p.n*
Ask us about Vietnam!

Everything seems implausibly cheap, given the distances involved.

It wasn't always like that. The Phillips family holidays were gruelling but are now a false happy memory, and when the Phillipses were gathered together they often spoke of them – the time Martin's canoe sank off the beach in Majorca, the time Tom was sick over a waiter in Corfu. Mr Phillips's favourite holiday had been on honeymoon in a cottage in Cornwall, hired via an old friend of Mr Phillips's father who ran a rental agency. The newly married Mr and Mrs Phillips had made love twenty-seven times in the week. Even then he had liked to count.

At the moment there is, or was, a plan to save enough to spend some time in the sunshine over the winter, a vision which appears to Mr Phillips as a girl's bottom, golden, with an almost invisible strip of cloth plunging vertiginously between her buttocks, an image all too familiar from TV but never seen in real life. It was a sight he felt he deserved to see at least once. This holiday is the first glimpse of a promised prosperity which in theory looms now that there is only one more year of payment left to go on the mortgage, thank God, and Martin has left home and Tom has only two years to go to official adulthood and the possibility of his leaving for college – though Mr Phillips somehow can't see that, since his younger son's pantomime defiance and self-sufficiency has within it, he feels, an unappeasable core of neediness. Tom isn't the moving-out type. Still, the Phillipses are, or should be, coming up to that stage in life where prosperity looms in front of middle-aged, middle-class couples like a plush, well-appointed antechamber to the grave, or a luxuriously fitted waiting room outside the offices of a doctor whose prognoses are exclusively fatal.

'What do you think you're doing, Phillips?'

Mr Phillips experiences momentarily and unpleasantly the sensation that his thoughts are legible to any passer-by. But no, this is simply Mr Tomkins, the bumptious co-founder of the local Neighbourhood Watch scheme, whose daughter Mrs Phillips coached to scraping a pass in Grade Four piano before she fell in love with her former gym teacher and emigrated to New Zealand. Tomkins's approach to the world had not changed. You had to give him credit for that. Or not, or something.

'A man can dream,' says Mr Phillips. Tomkins is wearing a suit that has at least three pieces and would perhaps turn out to have more under closer inspection. He works in a bank, turning down applicants for loans and overdrafts. Mr Phillips can imagine having a worse bank manager than Mr Tomkins, but only with difficulty.

'Off to work?'

'Men must work', says Tomkins, heading down the road towards the railway station, his furled umbrella swinging in his right hand on this dry day, 'and women must *shop*.' He has spoken over his shoulder and now he's gone.

Once Tomkins has cleared his own blast area, Mr Phillips

sets off after him. A crowd of people are getting on to a double-decker bus as he squeezes past. The street is blocked in both directions, as a fuming K-reg Mondeo has tried to squeeze past the bus, only to realize that the oncoming unloading laundry van doesn't offer enough room, and so the road is now officially chocka, at a standstill. The quickest moving things are pedestrians and a mad cyclist, dressed like a parody of a civil servant with bowler hat and cycle clips, dodging impatiently between the growling stationary vehicles. When he drives and gets stuck like that Mr Phillips has a vision of the whole city being locked in by immobile traffic, a pattern of stalled and blocked-in vehicles ramifying and spreading like a pattern of crystals growing under a microscope, so that the jam – a totally solid gridlock, not just slow-moving but fixed – gradually spreads all over the capital, junctions clogging, back flows building up, a cancer of stasis blocking every traffic light, intersection, box junction, mini-roundabout, square and one-way system, the whole city gradually and permanently shutting down like a dying brain.

Mr Phillips, his return ticket tucked in his jacket pocket like a handkerchief, stands on the platform at Clapham Junction and waits for his train. It's already getting warmer, and it's possible to wish that he had worn a lighter suit. Even his briefcase looks as if it might be beginning to sweat. Along the platform a straggling line of fellow commuters is ready to rush the next train, and is filling the time by reading newspapers, though there are variant activities too – a girl in a knee-length split skirt nodding her head as she listens to a walkman, and a few oddbods reading books. Mr Phillips has not taken his book out of his case; he prefers to watch and wait. Next to him on one side a very tall man in jeans and a T-shirt is reading the *Daily Sport*, stopping at every other page to inspect with real care the pictures of naked women, all of whom to Mr Phillips's eyes have breasts that are implausibly large and unerotically rigid, as if they had been inflated especially for the occasion. Not for the first time Mr Phillips wonders who these girls are.

He does a calculation: the papers publish say seventy pictures of girls with no clothes on a week – a highly conservative figure, given that there's one every day in the *Sun*, one in the *Mirror*, seven in the *Sport*, one in the *Star*, plus say another dozen on Sundays, which comes to seventy-two. So that's 72 times 52 naked girls a year, which is 70 times 50 is 3500 plus 70 times two is 140 is 3640 plus two times 52 is 104 is 3744 naked girls in the newspapers. Then magazines, dirty magazines *per se*, there are dozens: *Fiesta*, *Men Only*, *Knave*, *Penthouse*, *Playboy*, *Mayfair*, also specialist magazines, *Asian Babes*, big tit mags, fat girl mags, *Readers' Wives*, you name it; so assume, again super-conservatively, at least twenty-five magazines coming out every week, with say ten girls per issue each, which would probably be more if you allow for smaller pictures in the personals, round-ups, last year's greatest hits etc, but say ten per issue, which is 25 x 10 = 250 naked girls per week times 52 is 50 times 250 is 12500 plus 2 times 250 is 500 = 13000. When you add the newspaper figure this gives a very very conservative estimate of 3744 plus 13000 = 16744, which is the number of British women happy to take their clothes off for money per annum. All of them, except the specialist interest ones, have bodies like the girl in the photograph that the man has now stopped looking at as he turns the page to begin reading a piece called 'Hanky-Panky No Thanky! Neighbours' Spanking Game Keeps Street Up All Night'.

Seventeen thousand people would be a town one and a half times the size of St Ives, where they took their first holiday after Martin was born. So that's a whole small townful of naked British women among us disguised as normal people. For a moment Mr Phillips is distracted by the idea of his town of nude women going through the day with no men anywhere about, going to do the shopping, washing things, sitting in offices, cleaning windows on those terrifying lift gadgets, their breasts and bums jiggling, some of them looking distinctly chilly which of course makes them go all shivery and pointy-nippled. Did they feel nervous the day the photos came out, of being recognized in the street; or proud, boasting to friends and family? Of course, being recognized could be embarrassing for other people too. I'm sure I know you from somewhere, Mrs Whatsit. Honestly for the life of me I'm quite sure you're mistaken, Vicar.

Seventeen thousand naked women was a lot of naked women. More than enough for most purposes. Mr Phillips thinks often about what it would be like to have a harem. If you thought about it too much, of course, you would start to become aware of all the possible complications, so the thing was to keep the fantasy as pure as possible: restrict it to the idea of women on tap for sex, as much sex as you wanted, all the time, variety and strangeness freely sanctioned, available. Yum yum! And of course the women would not be women but girls, since that is what men mostly want, all attempts to pretend otherwise notwithstanding. Indeed, one of the first signs of growing older was when you stopped fancying older women. The desperate heat with which Mr Phillips had looked at his teachers, younger friends of his mother's, anyone, is a still vivid memory. The fantasy was about being taken to bed by an older woman. Mrs Robinson, that was the general idea. 'Seduced' was the usual word but it was a bad word since it implied reluctance on the part of him, Mr Phillips. It suggested that he was done unto when all he wanted was to be done. He enters no claims for the originality of the fantasy.

Then he began to notice much younger women, schoolgirls even, sixteen perhaps, but who knew? It's as if there was one specific moment when you switched from one sort of sexual fantasies to another: you went off to work one day thinking about Anne Bancroft in *The Graduate* and you came back thinking about Jenny Agutter in *The Railway Children*. Or perhaps there was a brief, blessed interlude of fancying both or neither, in the way that some men were randy for all women all the time and others seemed to live in a cocoon of sexlessness – which in so many ways would make life simpler. It would be like living in a completely flat country with brilliant public transport and amenities and nothing to complain about.

Eventually, with sadness, he recognized this fantasy switch as a sign of ageing: his genes wanted to impregnate some good young breeding stock and thereby allow their vehicle, his body, to go out on a high note. As far as Mr Phillips is concerned, that's the beauty of genes, you can blame them for almost anything. The voice inside which says *Get a younger one* is like the moment in the film where Sean Connery is a policeman investigating a sex crime and he says to his wife, 'Why aren't you beautiful?' Beautiful here was another word for young.

Mr Phillips can remember what must have been almost his first time, the onset of the Younger Woman. She had been a barmaid at the Frog and Parrot on a quiz night about twenty years before, the days when he used to do that sort of thing.

She was reaching down to stack glasses on a circular rack inside a dish-washer, her long skirt riding slightly at her waist, her way of folding herself up into a crouch somehow impossible, like origami. Mr Phillips had felt an awful gust of her youth sweep over him, a pure lust to penetrate and corrupt. What was it Tony Curtis said, when asked the secret of eternal youth? 'The saliva of girls.' The next thing you knew you were slowing down as you drove past bus stops.

So the harem would have girls for sex. But thinking more, you realized it could not stop there. You would need someone to cook, like Mrs Mitchinson whom Mr Phillips had worked with at Grimshaw's and who was forever talking about, thinking about, shopping for and cooking, food. Her husband was a small, round, very silent man who always seemed to be smiling. Mr Phillips had only eaten her food twice and still remembered it – not that it was fancy or elaborate, roast chicken and apple tart the once, fish cakes and home-made ice cream the next, but so vivid, like alchemy. As for the sex part, it wasn't what you would first think of with Mrs Mitchinson, she was low and round like her husband, with a bright red face, one of those Russian dolls, but it would be clearly part of the deal and you would have to keep your side of the bargain, not every night of course, that was the whole point of the harem arrangement, but at least every six months or so. Although perhaps you would have an off-limits granny or two, to keep order and boss the servants (who would be part of the harem too) and help with the inevitable baby-sitting. He would have his secretary Karen, obviously, to help with accounts and household expenses (Mrs Phillips would appreciate that), but also for sex, perhaps at the same time, having her bent over the desk and straightening out papers afterwards – not something Mr Phillips had thought about less than ten thousand times. He would have that Clarissa Colingford, you needed a touch of glamour. Sharon Mitchell would be a blast from the past. Perhaps Tricia the cleaning lady. There would be Superman's girlfriend, from the TV series, he couldn't remember her name. But Mrs Phillips would always be wife number one. He owed her that.

A train, one of the small, boxy, graceless, modern commuter types, appears around the bend four hundred yards away and slows into the station. The platformful of passengers assembles around the doors, which wheeze open in a row, and a few dozen people hop out of their carriages, minding the gap, before a couple of hundred others surge onto the train. Like most experienced commuters, Mr Phillips has a variety of techniques for seizing somewhere to sit, sneaking in around the side of the door and sliding into one of the jump-seats or barrelling down to the far end of the compartment, through the thickets of passengers, briefcases, newspapers, outstretched legs. Today though he is content to strap-hang, or not worked-up enough to fight for a seat. The battle for a space prepared you for, was an allegory or image of, the daily struggle. You could argue that those who fought their way to the seats were the people who needed them least. To them that hath shall be given, that was the deal.

Clinging to his metal post by the door Mr Phillips looks around the compartment and wonders if he is the only person here who isn't on his way to work. Eighty percent of the men in the compartment are wearing suits and ties. They all look tired. Office people heading in to work look tired at the beginning of the day and febrilely energetic, in a hurry to escape, on the way home. It's as if the thought of work drains them of vigour whereas leaving work gives them a jolt of it. Mr Phillips is no stranger to that feeling himself: his heart is always lighter on the trip down the steps from Clapham Junction at the end of the day than on the trip up them at the beginning.

A young man sits across from him in jeans and a black T-shirt with the words *Rage Against the Machine* written on it. He chews gum mechanically, like a cow chewing the cud, and he is stubbly, looking into space; perhaps he isn't going in to work. But no, the gum chewer reaches into a back pocket and takes out a tiny mobile phone. Like every mobile phone conversation Mr Phillips has ever heard, this call is largely about the fact of its own occurrence. He wants to eavesdrop on people saying 'Sell, sell, sell! Unload it all now!' or 'What do you mean, am I fucking Janet?' or 'It's *you* who's the spoilt one!' but all he ever hears is 'I'm at the bus stop / in the street / on the mobile / on my way / late / early / nearly there' or as in this case:

'Yeah – me. Yeah, I'm on the train. Yeah, be there in plenty of time, we've just left the Junction. Yeah, bye.' The youth puts the mobile back into his pocket and wriggles his buttocks on the plastic train seat in a pleased way. Mr Phillips feels a moment of loathing hit him like indigestion.

No sooner has the train accelerated for forty seconds or so than it begins to slow down. The terrain outside has the low, scruffy, nowhere-in-particular feel of generic South London: a furniture warehouse, the backs of houses, a Baptist church. On the other side of the train tracks a billboard directed at returning commuters says 'If you lived here you'd be at home by now.' A few passengers put newspapers away, arrange their bits and pieces and prepare to push towards the doors or brace themselves in preparation for standing up.

The train squeals to a halt, people get off, and further knackered-looking people in work uniform get on. Mr Phillips is a non-combatant, he again doesn't enter the contest for seats. The train is properly crowded now. A thin, pointy-faced woman in spinster's clothes, close to Mr Phillips's age, has insinuated herself between him and the wall of smeared transparent plastic that separates the standing-room-only door area from the seats and the rest of the compartment.

Mr Phillips takes the view that many human capacities – courage, strength, will-power, luck, sex-appeal – are finite, that you draw against an unreplenishable fund of them like capital left in a bank, so that when they've gone they're gone for ever. Today is one of those days when he feels that his capacity for self-assertion is finite, so that if he uses some up now he may not have any available later.

We condition ourselves very hard to screen out the details of our enforced city intimacies. Oh, but it's hard sometimes. Today

Mr Phillips can smell the heated deodorant of the pole-gripping man standing next to him, the armpit-warmed chemical odour of what at the boys' school was called 'Poof Spray'. He can see the grain on the skin of a girl standing eighteen inches away from him reading the problem page of a folded magazine and see also the slight psoriatic redness and scurf where her hair is scraped thinly upwards at the nape of her neck. Two walkmen are competing in the standing area, both tinny and tinnitic, their owners a black boy in a sweatshirt and a white woman with purple lipstick. Martin says that walkmen are the worst thing you can do for your hearing, so both these people are presumably going deaf, though not quickly and completely enough to suit Mr Phillips. The noise always makes him think of insects.

Although there is a gust of new oxygen when the train doors open, the air inside the compartment feels as if it has been breathed and rebreathed, recycled through lungs, picking up bacilli, viruses, tiny minute droplets of mucus and lining and bad breath and stomach gases, the feet and farts and crotch-whiffs of everyone in the train, going round and round their respiratory systems before being passed on to the next commuter. It's like that story about the water in London having been through three people's urinary tracts before it's finally drunk (which Mr Phillips has seen denounced as a fiction by a bald man from the water company, the same one who was always going on about how little water there was in the reservoirs). But even if it wasn't true it felt true and tasted true, and even more so for the air.

Looking at the number of people in here, it simply does not seem possible that there is enough oxygen to go around. Especially if the train stops – which now, as Mr Phillips is thinking these thoughts, it does. London trains have many different kinds of stop: a tremulous, we-could-be-off-at-any-moment, champing-at-the-bit kind of stop (often very deceptive, since the train can stay in this condition for minutes, even hours); the exhausted, clanking, what-is-it-this-time, why-won't-the-others-get-out-of-my-tunnel, never-quite-getting-up-to-full-speed-without-coming-to-a-halt-a-few-seconds-later stop (which can give the feeling that a secret mechanism forces the train to stop for a specified number of minutes every time it exceeds a certain speed); the much feared, horribly disconcerting total blackout mid-tunnel stop; and, as in this case, the heavy, final, definitive quiet of the stop that makes it clear right from the outset that it's going to be a long one. It is impossible not to speculate about what has happened. A suicide? Surely not in rush hour. Nobody could be that thoughtless. A mechanical failure? And if so, what kind – malfunctioning signal, erratic signal light, wonky track, broken-down train, power cut? Or something cataclysmic, like a fire? Thank God they aren't underground, in a tunnel. (Mr Phillips's personal record stuck underground is an hour and a half.) The supply of oxygen wouldn't be infinite, that stood to reason, so just how finite was it?

Perhaps the most oppressive thing is the silence, not just the silence of the train but the silence inside the compartment.

Quite a few people must be experiencing acute discomfort – choking fantasies, oxygen terrors, panics about fainting, urgent intimations of imminent mortality, detailed scenarios about passing out, falling, knocking their heads and pissing themselves – but no one shows it. This in its way is as unnerving as if people were bursting into tears and shouting 'We're all going to die!' It is a more British version of the same thing.

Mr Phillips can feel himself swaying and bouncing with the blood supply to his feet. Somewhere in the world there are yogis and fakirs and shamen who have the ability to banish this sort of thing from their minds. He tries to make himself drift off into thinking about his imaginary Neighbourhood Watch meeting. But it just isn't comfortable enough inside the train compartment, which is hot both with the sunlight and with the body heat of people in suits. The girl with scraped-back hair is looking pink with the warmth, and she isn't the only one. At the offices of Wilkins and Co., where the windows can't be opened and the air-conditioning doesn't work properly, it will be an uncomfortable day with even Mr Mill's secretary, saintly shy Janet, looking like she wouldn't mind doing a bit of complaining. In summer she wears sleeveless dresses which give you glimpses of armpit and sometimes the preliminary foothills of flesh swelling like the lower slopes of a volcano at the side of her breasts.

The train judders into motion again and Mr Phillips decides on impulse to get off. After all, it's not as if I'm going anywhere. Every single person on this train is going to work

except me, thinks Mr Phillips, but then he squashes the
thought down with an almost physical effort and as he does so
pictures to himself an elephant sitting on a small mound of
cardboard boxes and flattening them, with bits of polystyrene
exploding everywhere.

The spires of Battersea Power Station loom up over the rail tracks ahead and Mr Phillips realizes where he is, at the stop close by Battersea Dogs' Home. This is a place where commuters get on rather than off – even though a few people must of course come here to look after the dogs, fix their little meals, check them for fleas and talk up their virtues to prospective owners. 'He's got a very sweet nature,' they would say of famously grumpy compulsive biters, or 'very affectionate' of the neurotically ungrateful mutt who pretends not to recognize anybody. And then the dogs are put down if they can't find a home after a specific length of time. He wonders if they get fond of particular dogs that can't find a home, ugly dogs or dogs with bad breath and limps and chewed-off ears, and there's a countdown to when they have to be put down so that the attempts to find an owner become increasingly desperate, and then the dreadful day of the fatal injection dawns, so that apprentices and new workers at the Home have to be taken to one side on the first day and told, 'Never get too close to a dog.'

The train lurches to a stop and Mr Phillips gets off. It's cooler outside, so there's an immediate feeling of relief. It's self-conscious-making, getting off in a suit and tie and sexy black briefcase in this un-officey part of London, but no one seems to notice. We wouldn't care so much what people thought of us if we knew how seldom they did. Mrs Phillips used to say that to the boys when they were preoccupied with some schoolboy issue of declining popularity or he-said-I-said-he-said. A temperamental difference was made apparent by this advice. To Mr Phillips the fact of others' indifference has never brought any comfort.

Further along the platform three girls have also got off the train and are heading for the station exit. It isn't a school-day so it's no surprise that they don't have a school look about them. They're a classic plain-pretty combination with an extra girl thrown in for ballast: a dumpy, brown-haired girl on the right with baggy jeans worn hanging off her hips so that a two-inch roll of flesh is visible all round her midriff; a tall girl with very straight blonde hair wearing a white T-shirt cut to show off her middle and a grey sort-of-towelling tracksuit bottom with a folded-over elasticized waistband. Mr Phillips can't see her face but she must be pretty as two of the male worker bees hurtling up the stairs on to the train give her a sideways once-over as they scramble for the closing doors. Mr Phillips finds it impossible to look at her narrow back without wondering what it would be like to lick (salty but in a good way, is his best guess). The third girl is wearing a black shell suit with blue stripes and heavy trainers. Their assumed air of toughness makes them look even younger than they are – sixteen, if that.

As the train pulls out a gust of air sweeps newspaper pages

and other litter along the platform. Mr Phillips trots down the stairs and leaves the station. The three girls have already vanished. Mr Phillips thinks for a moment about heading down the road towards Vauxhall, the way he would go if he were driving into work, past the new MI6 headquarters and Lambeth Palace and St Thomas's hospital where Martin and Thomas were born, along to Waterloo and then across to Southwark Bridge. Instead he turns left and heads towards Battersea Park, catching for a moment, during a gap in traffic, unless he's imagining it, the sound of forlorn woofings and bayings from the Dogs' Home down the road.

It is warm in the direct sunlight down at street level. The traffic makes it feel even warmer. Mr Phillips undoes the top button of his shirt and gives his tie a slight downward loosening tug. This is a gesture he has seen in films, indicating freedom and/or fatigue. A truck attempting an illegal right turn blocks the traffic, and Mr Phillips crosses the road in a black cloud of belched diesel fumes. At this time of the day London is all about traffic. In the mostly stationary cars people behave as if they can't be observed, and because their cars are a private space they tend to behave as if they are in private. What this means in practice is that a very large number of them are picking their noses. Mr Phillips has noticed this before but today the syndrome is especially apparent: in the two hundred yards between the railway station and the park he passes three people picking their noses, all with an air of Zen-like calm. Is this sample statistically significant for how much nose-picking goes on in normal circumstances – in which case Mr Phillips feels a little left out – or is it something that people do especially when they're driving?

When he finally gets into the park Mr Phillips, after nearly being run over by a rollerblader travelling 20 mph faster than any car he has seen so far today, crosses the outer ring road and heads towards the sound of screeching peacocks. A man in a tracksuit with a very tanned face is practising juggling with torches. A jogger, a tall man wearing white shorts who has a curious prancing stride, lifting his knees high, passes Mr Phillips and gives him a sidelong look as he bounces by. Presumably you don't see many people in suits carrying briefcases in parks at this time of the day.

At the peacock enclosure a small crowd has gathered to watch the birds. One of the males is displaying, his tail fanned out in too many varieties of blue to name. To Mr Phillips, the intricate pattern of colours would be purely beautiful if it weren't for the eye motif imprinted on the tail. The hen peacock is sort-of-not-looking but hasn't wandered away, and the other peacocks and peahens are minding their own business. There is something ridiculous about the male's display, the lengths to which the bird is having to go to attract attention – but then there always is about males trying to seize the notice of females, whether it's to do with banging your head against another stag after a 40 mph run-up or simply wearing black clothes and trying to look fascinatingly uninterested in an irresistibly interesting way. Part of Martin's success with girls must be to do with his mastery of this proactive, highly visible and sexually signalling form of looking bored. And then, he is tremendously good at smoking. That has been an asset too. It's so often men's desire not to look ridiculous that makes them look ridiculous.

One of the men standing looking at the peacocks is another jogger, who is holding on to the wire fence and doing stretching exercises while making short puffing exhalations. There are two different sets of woman-and-pram-and-baby combinations, one of them apparently a Filipina nanny and the other either a youngish mother dressed down or an oldish, poshish nanny. An old couple with a small energetic dog, some make of terrier, have stopped for a look and a breather. They are wearing roughly twice as many clothes as everyone else, as old people often do. Mr Phillips is feeling hot in his suit with the buttons undone, but this couple are wearing coats and, in the man's case, a little tweed hat. One of them will die before the other.

The peacock is making a half-turn now, as if to try and bounce the sunlight off his fan of feathers. He is cawing loudly, giving it all he's got. Mr Phillips, a regular weekend visitor to the park when the children were small, knows the sound well. Sometimes the cry is like a cat miaowing or caterwauling, the male's penis abrading the female and triggering its ovulation with the shocking withdrawal of the tom's penis-bristles. Mr Phillips likes that sound, just as he has always liked overhearing other people make love, especially the mousy-looking couple who had lived next to Mr Phillips and Mrs Phillips at their first marital home. That was a terraced house in Bromley where the sound of the short, shy wife noisily climaxing in a choked wail was a regular feature. It was often bizarrely late, at one or two in the morning; did they wake up and decide to do it, was it an attempt to circumvent insomnia, or were they so self-conscious about the noise that they deliberately tried to stay awake and waited to do it in the vain hope that their neighbours might be asleep? In any case Mr Phillips never saw or thought of them without a sharp jab of envy. Sometimes when Mrs Phillips is away or out he puts a glass to the wall in an attempt to catch the Cartwrights or the Cotts at it. No luck so far. *No one ever does it.* Mr Phillips decides now that the peacock could also sound like a female voice saying 'No', or 'Help'.

Mr Phillips wanders off past the peacock enclosure and heads in the direction of the lake. Two sweepers, one black and one white, are standing leaning on their brushes talking with their heads very close together in a gesture charged with a sense of secrecy and importance. Beyond them the pond is a muddy grey colour, the shore stained with the white smear of shit left by Canada geese.

A few people are already on the lake, splashing about in hired boats. The men in them are all trying not to look as bad at rowing as they are.

When he was training as an accountant Mr Phillips had fallen in love with the double entry book system. It seemed suddenly a whole new language in which to describe the world; or rather it suddenly seemed as if the world was describable in a new and better way. Things became more clear, more starkly lit. That was soothing. For a few weeks he had done an impromptu double entry account for everything from his personal finances to his parent's house and belongings to Crystal Palace Football Club (where players were automatically listed under assets, a debatable point to fans but an ineluctable decision in the crystalline logic of the accountant). Now, walking in Battersea Park Mr Phillips feels the long suppressed need to draw up a tranquillizing double entry. The thing to imagine was that the park suddenly ceased to function as a going concern, and all its assets and liabilities were frozen in the moment of disposal.

ASSETS	LIABILITIES
Fees from people willing to pay to shoot geese	Cost of geese damage
	Upkeep of pavements
Park benches	Subventions from Wandsworth Council
Rent from park-keeper's cottage	Salaries of park keepers, park police
Fees for tennis courts, football pitches, etc.	Insurance for trips and falls
Money from recycled bottles	Bottle bank recycling gear upkeep
Car park fees	Car park upkeep

ASSETS	LIABILITIES
Paint, etc., in storage	*Peacock upkeep, feed, etc.*
Tulips, etc., to sell	*Fertilizer costs*
Feed, etc., in storage	*Storage upkeep, sheds, etc.*
Golden Buddha	*Upkeep of Buddha, gilt paint, etc.*
Fees from special events	*Cost of setting them up*
Film fees	*Upkeep of cricket pitches, bowling lawns, etc.*
Boat fees	*Pollution monitoring in pond*
Statues, monuments, sculptures	*Upkeep thereof*

There were bound to be lots of other things he hadn't thought of. It would cost a fair old bit, running a park.

Mr Phillips walks past the pond and along the road that curves around the park. Every few seconds a cyclist, rollerblader or jogger floats, cruises or puffs by him. The very sight of this is tiring. Mr Phillips in general doesn't mind exertion all that much, but he dislikes the idea of it. Any kind of effort weighs on his spirits in advance, he can feel it coming. It's like the fatigue he experiences at the beginning of a day that he knows in advance will be long and boring, so that it's as if the whole eight or ten or twenty hours of ennui are crushed and compacted into every single moment. The anticipation of a gruelling day always makes him feel like Superman confronted by a villain wielding a lump of Kryptonite.

In front of him a small boy is whacking the fence beside the tennis court with a stick while his mother trails along behind, also carrying a stick, which she is running more slowly and meditatively over the bars of the same fence, as if playing a musical instrument visible only to her. Like many young parents she wears the glazed and disconnected look of a combat soldier.

Mr Phillips stops beside the tennis court to rest for a moment. There is nowhere to sit down except two small benches immediately beside the courts. He feels too self-conscious to go that close so he puts down his briefcase, takes off his jacket and stands watching. As soon as he stops walking he becomes conscious of a light breeze.

The three courts are occupied by, from left to right, a father and son combination of about forty and ten years old, the father hitting patronizingly gentle forehands to his concentrating offspring; two girls in their late teens in short white dresses and long dark-blue socks, playing competitively and seriously; and a middle aged mixed doubles outfit, well matched and cunning but slightly heavy on their feet. Mr Phillips concentrates his attention on the girls while pretending to pay attention to the other two pairs – in other words he holds his head pointing in one direction or the other while secretly keeping his eyes on the middle. One girl's dress rides up when she serves to show a glimpse of legs all the way up to her bum. Her legs and arms are the colour of Weetabix. She's blonde and has a ponytail which flops about her head and shoulders as she moves. They both look as if tennis is a big thing for them. Mr Phillips wonders if they change ends after two games and if so whether he has the nerve to stay around long enough to get a better look at the darker girl.

'It's Wimbledon that brings them out,' says a man beside Mr Phillips. The newcomer, a short, fair businessman type with strange grey eyes, is standing with his hands in the pockets of a green suit. On second glance he doesn't look as much like a businessman as something more louche and selfish.

'I'm sorry?' says Mr Phillips.

'Wimbledon – you can't get on the courts for weeks afterwards. It's the end of July now, we'll have at least another fortnight before the effect wears off.'

The man falls silent again and stands beside Mr Phillips watching the tennis. His presence makes Mr Phillips feel more rather than less self-conscious and he begins regretfully to contemplate walking away from the tennis courts. The darker-haired girl, who has breasts that are of a nice human scale, not at all like the girls in the magazines, is changing ends and walking towards them. She looks up at them for a moment, a glance from under her eyelashes in the manner copyrighted by Princess Diana, and Mr Phillips feels his penis twitch.

'The thing I like most about Wimbledon,' says the man, 'is watching the girl players fish the balls out from their knickers when they're about to serve. Isn't that your favourite thing too?'

'What?' says Mr Phillips.

'I said, standards in the women's game and the simultaneous raising of the velocity of the men's game, especially as played on grass, because of racket technology, have meant that the women's game, on grass at least, is now more interesting to watch than the men's, don't you find?'

'No, you didn't,' says Mr Phillips. 'You said something about the balls being all lovely and warm when they came out of the players' knickers.'

The man looks expressionlessly at him for a moment and then laughs a rich relaxed laugh that smells faintly of last night's alcohol. He seems to flop or slump slightly as he reaches into an inside pocket and takes out a glinting object that for a hallucinatory split second Mr Phillips thinks is a gun but is in fact a silver case carrying skinny cigars. The man offers the case, opened like a book, to Mr Phillips, who declines. He then takes a cigar for himself and lights it with a metal Zippo lighter that leaves behind it a whiff of lighter fluid.

'Shocking habit,' says the man. 'Unless that's a contradiction in terms. These are Cuban, rolled on the thighs of virgins and all that. Ideally they should be roughly three times this size. The bigger ones have more flavour. Like women, I hear you think.'

'I was thinking nothing of the sort,' says Mr Phillips.

'Aha. More on the little girls side of things, are we? You must be, what, early fifties? The younger the chicken the sweeter the pickin', the older the fiddle the sweeter the tune, am I right? Slowing down as you drive past bus stops, that sort of thing?'

'Mind your own business,' says Mr Phillips, pushing back from the railings and beginning to walk off towards the river. The man picks up his, Mr Phillips's, briefcase and begins to come after him.

'Steady on, no offence I hope,' he says, still friendly. 'I *am* minding my business. In fact you could even say that I am working. Hang on a minute, you've forgotten your case.'

'Thank you,' says Mr Phillips, stopping to take the proffered bag. The man pretends to snatch it back and then lets him take it.

'Magazine publishing. Top shelf. London Publishing Company Inc., Mr Fortesque, Managing Director.' Now the man is offering a card, which Mr Phillips takes. It says the same things as the man has just said.

'I like to come to the park to get ideas,' says the man, joining Mr Phillips at a strolling pace. 'Basic research. I come here, look around, look at girls, look at men looking at girls, try and cook up some ideas based on what I see. Tennis now: there's a thought. A whole magazine based on girls playing tennis – girls leaning over showing their bums, glimpses of tit when they throw up the ball, that sort of thing. Story ideas: the lesbian initiation in the locker room. It's a well-known fact that half of them are big-time dykes. A whole series of stories right there: first time, two on one, the shower scene, rivals kissing and making up and making out, suggestive use of rackets, all this is just off the top of my head. Prose narratives as well as picture layouts. Letters from readers, maybe we'd even get the occasional genuine one every now and again, with anecdotes

and reminiscences and suggestions for future issues. The figure of the tennis coach, something for the ladies. You could do
something with readers' wives, too – amateur stuff, very
nineties. The beauty of that is the worse it is the better, up to a
point anyway. I can judge that point. That's what experience
means. It's as valuable in this game as in any other. Niche mar-
kets. This whole Asian babes, fat girls, thin girls, big tits, teen
totty, it's been as far as it goes and we're ready for the next big
thing. That could be specialization by jobs and milieu – not
just tennis players but nurses, policewomen, traffic wardens,
secretaries. Let's face it, why do you think people watch tennis
on the telly in the first place? To get new ideas about the place-
ment and timing of their forehands? Bollocks. It's for the totty.
It's basically about women's knickers. They should have a
camera trained on them as they serve, a super-slow motion
Knicker-Cam. Or Totty-Cam? You have to give people what
they want. Think of that photo with the girl's skirt hitched up
and her rubbing her bum. Just a glimpse of cheek, that's all
you really get – but what a classic. Not that it makes much
sense. Is she supposed to have been hit on the arse by the ball,
or what? And why isn't she wearing any knickers? Go bril-
liantly in a story shoot, that would.'

'I used to fancy my secretary,' admits Mr Phillips. They have
gone as far as the Thames and are looking across the river
towards Chelsea. He came here with Mrs Phillips when they
were courting. 'It's like a Canaletto,' she had said, and he had
agreed, not having the faintest idea who Canaletto was. Now he

did know, and although he didn't think it was particularly true, he knows what she meant, and in any case always thinks of it when he sees that stretch of trees and houses and riverbank.

'Of course you did. Everybody fancies their secretary. That's what offices are all about.'

'I often used to wonder if she thought about me in the same way,' says Mr Phillips, truthfully. There are whole parts of sexy Karen's mind that are wholly unguessable to him – which was of course a large component of what made her sexy.

'Why speak in the past tense? I'm sure she's thinking about you right now. Not that it matters. Speaking as a pornographer, I can tell you that the important thing is never to try and work out what a woman is thinking. It only confuses you and they change their minds so much anyway the main thing is just to steam ahead with your plan intact.'

'I lost my job', says Mr Phillips.

'Why else would you be wandering around Battersea Park at half past nine on a work day? Naturally you haven't told your wife and family,' says the man.

'No, I haven't'.

'And this was – last week? Last month? Last October?'

'Friday,' says Mr Phillips.

'Friday!'

'Friday morning.'

The man smokes for a while, looking at an unladen barge heading up the Thames. More dangerous than it looks; if you fall in you're dead in no time.

'It's always a shocker,' says the pornographer. 'I haven't been sacked for years – it's one of the perks of being your own boss – but in the days when I worked for other people it used to happen all the time. I've been sacked for being drunk, for being chronically late, for being lazy, and then for planning to nick personnel and ideas and set up my own company – which was justified, incidentally. But then so were all the others. In retrospect, mind – I'm not claiming that's what I felt at the time. But when they sacked me for disloyalty, instead of being something I was thinking about doing it became something I had to do, and the next thing you know I was my old firm's biggest competitor. They publish traditional tit mags – still stuck in the seventies, basically.' He ponders his own success for a moment, and then says in a different tone, 'Mind you, even when you see it coming it's an upset.'

'I can't say that I saw it coming,' says Mr Phillips. And this was true. One of his least favourite parts of the job, as deputy chief of accounts at Wilkins and Co., had been preparing breakdowns of the cost of making employees redundant. This was something he did in concert with Mr Somers, the deputy head of the legal department. You checked the contract and did the sums. Then, inevitably, you bumped into the person about whom you had just been preparing the figures. Once Mr Phillips had spent an hour stuck in a lift with a man from the marketing department whose sacking he had been costing that very morning. His contract meant he was due six months' pay, so it wasn't cheap – though as Mr Mill, the drunk, idle and unreliable head of accounts, was wont to point out, 'There's always money for redundancies.' In the stationary lift they had talked about football for most of the hour, until some firemen came, apologizing for being so slow but saying they'd had to come via a chip pan blaze at a nurses' hostel in Holborn.

Someone in accounts must have run a ruler over his own dismissal, he realizes. It couldn't have been Monroe, since they would have known that Monroe would have told him and in any case he couldn't have kept it secret, given that they shared an office. It wouldn't have been Mr Mill, who wasn't up to anything more complicated than the two times table, and even that only before lunch. If they were looking for highish-level redundancies in accounts, Mill was lucky not to have been sacked himself. But as a director of the company he was on a year's notice, and therefore prohibitively expensive to sack, notwithstanding his own rule. Mr Phillips's old partner in crime Mr Somers must have known. Not that Mr Phillips would have been expensive or complicated to sack, with a straightforward three-month notice period and no tricky nonsense over bonus schemes or anything like that. They had promised to pay his pension contributions for two years or until he got another job, whichever was sooner. So this was it: redundancy.

The interview or meeting or conversation with Mr Wilkins, the managing director, at which the news was broken, had been like a flashback to school and the time he was caned for being part of a group who smashed some windows in an after-hours throw-a-rock-over-the-gym competition. On that occasion the headmaster had not actually said the words 'This is going to hurt me more than it hurts you,' but the sentiment was implicit in his pained, actorish demeanour. Mr Wilkins was like that too. Mr Phillips, once he realized what the purpose of the meeting was – which didn't take long – was in a state of complete numbness and only heard the gist of what the company's eponymous paramount chief had to say.

'Unexpected lingering effects of recession among customers in our market sector –'

Wilkins and Co. was a catering services supply company.

'– gap between revenue and provisions – retrenchments called for – not a case of so-called "downsizing" for its own sake – company policy of exacting cuts department by department – accountancy's turn to "give" – as always in these cases no question of any implied comment on the ability of anyone involved – he himself had once – best thing that ever – absolute confidence that – Wilkins and Co.'s settled policy of trying to act as generously as possible in these instances – one of the many ways in which the company tried to behave as a progressive, humane employer –'

As with many energetic talkers Mr Wilkins seemed as keen to convince himself as the person to whom he was talking. The point about Wilkins and Co. being enlightened employers seemed especially important to him.

'– not necessary to serve out full notice period – inevitable

sense of gloom on these occasions – fresh fields and pastures
new – better for all concerned – particularly keen that depart-
ing employees should get to keep their company cars at competitive terms – not a relevant factor in this particular case –
these little and not-so-little things which make all the difference – Mr Phillips's valuable contribution to Wilkins and Co. –
once part of the team always part of the team – importance of
team players like Mr Phillips to any company – regret and also
sadness and also sense of new beginnings – not the least service he had performed the company his current bearing under
difficult circumstances – was that the time – another meeting –
thank you thank you.'

When Mr Phillips had first gone to Wilkins and Co. in 1969,
Mr Wilkins, the son of the founder, had then been young to be
the managing director of a company of that size. He had one of
those tanks full of heavy pink oil which slosh from side to side
in a supposedly soothing way. It was what they used to call an
executive toy. Nowadays his office was decorated with two
abstract paintings. The photos of his family which sat on his
desk were turned towards the visitor's seat, either because Mr
Wilkins was sick of the sight of them and/or because he
wanted to show them off. So the last thing Mr Phillips saw as
he left his now ex-employer's office was a picture of his boss's
son wearing robes and smiling nervously in a graduation day
studio portrait.

Mr Phillips went back to his office and slumped into his
chair, which wheezed out a puff of air, as if it and not he were

making a physical effort. Neither Mr Monroe nor Karen was there. For some time he sat and didn't do anything. No one came into his office and the telephone did not ring. Then he leaned forward, took a pencil out of the 'World's Greatest Dad' mug he had bought himself one Father's Day and began to do some sums.

'You're a what?' asks the man in the park.

'I'm not an anything now,' says Mr Phillips.

'That's no way to think.'

'But it's true.'

'Ah, "but what is truth?" I've always thought that wasn't nearly as clever a remark as it's supposed to be. It's like those wankers who say "Define your terms" when you're having an argument, like a record with a broken needle. There's no excuse for anyone over the age of fifteen using that kind of trick in argument. So you're a what?'

'I'm an accountant,' says Mr Phillips.

'I'm good at sums myself,' says the man. 'Not like these days with the calculators at school, you'd wonder if they can even add up.'

'I use, used, a calculator all the time at work.' Mr Phillips has a twinge of romantic feeling about the calculator that prints out the figures fed through it, keeping track of any errors in the calculation. He has always privately thought of the calculator as surrounded by a nimbus of professional glamour, as much a symbol of the accountant's mystery as a stethoscope is a doctor's.

'What sort of accountant? City firm, that sort of thing?'

'I used to work for a catering supply company,' says Mr Phillips.

The man nods sympathetically. 'Wrong game. Can happen to anyone. Dual streams of revenue, that's the beauty of the magazine business. You've got your income from cover sales as well as your money from advertising. As an accountant you'll appreciate the elegance of that. Plus, the business is based on masturbation, which is the steadiest source of revenue imaginable. People buy the magazine to have a wank, and people advertise in the magazine to get in touch with people who wank, and it's all the best business in the world, since everybody wanks. You don't often hear it discussed, but it's true. People always say the great taboo is death, but in my experience you hear death discussed a lot more than you do wanking. Perhaps older people don't do it quite so much but you can bet that even they do it every now and again. Probably even the Queen does it. Mind you, you've got to watch the demographics. Older women, for instance, appeal mainly to very young men – I dare say you remember. But very young men haven't got any money, have they? Bad demographic. I've heard it said that lesbians go for older women too,' the man added in a more thoughtful tone, 'but that's a bit off my patch. You have to stick with what you know.'

There's some truth in all this, Mr Phillips has to admit. He himself does it never less than once a week and often as much as three times: at home in bed, or upstairs in his den, which is his favourite because he can lock the door and get a magazine out, though it's true that he prefers the fully prone position available in bed to the semi-recline he can get with his beloved den Barcalounger. This would of course affect the 96.7 per cent figure for not having sex, if you included all forms of sex including with yourself. He sometimes used to masturbate in the toilet of his office at Wilkins and Co., when seized by an irresistible impulse or when Karen was looking particularly attractive – though it was less a spur of the moment thing than a question of the need building up over a couple of days, a familiar and pleasant pressure around his prostate, a warmth in the balls, which eventually reached the point where it demanded release. Women probably don't masturbate in the toilet at work, Mr Phillips feels. He is quietly confident about that one. He once even masturbated in the toilet at Thomas's school during a PTA meeting (his cock had been hard, he had come with appropriately teenage speed).

There must be lots of evidence of Martin and Tom's masturbating, to be found in their sheets and in the bins, not to mention pornography stashed in drawers and under mattresses, but Mr Phillips doesn't want to know about it, and anyway can't imagine formulating the detective procedures by which he might find out for himself. No, he definitely doesn't want to know. Would it be different if he had daughters? Probably – Mr Phillips has no difficulty in imagining himself as a knicker-sniffer and injuncter of boyfriends. With his sons he feels a systematic, deliberate incuriosity. He authoritatively shirked the task of educating them about sex. In Mr Phillips's view this was not news anyone wanted to hear from their parents. Leave it to school and to porn mags. After all, what does he know? His own father's instructions about sex had been a late-night five-minute monologue about 'the strength being sapped' – a highly cryptic allusion to the subject of wet dreams, as Mr Phillips realized about a decade later. At the time of this chat he had already been having wet dreams for over a year.

'I have to go now,' says Mr Phillips. 'It was good meeting you.' He thinks about offering to shake hands but the moment seems subtly wrong. He has had enough of the park. They have walked as far as the giant gilded Buddha on the embankment; there are four Buddhas up the stairs on the square plinth, three of them very bright in the morning sunlight. Mr Phillips looks up past the man at the nearest of the Buddhas. He is fast asleep while attendants gaze fondly down at him. He looks like a man who enjoys his sleep. Mr Phillips tries to think of any pictures of God or Christ asleep, but the only ones he can come up with concern the disciples panicking during the storm on Lake Galilee while Christ has a zizz.

'Cheerio,' says the man. 'I'm sorry you lost your job. You've got my number. Give me a call if you want to have another chat, or if you have any ideas for magazines.' As Mr Phillips wanders away he calls after him, 'And thanks for your input on the tennis thing.'

Mr Phillips stands on Chelsea Bridge and looks down at the Thames. Across the road, next to the ruins of Battersea Power Station, a man tied to an enormous rubber band is jumping from a crane.

Presumably the less safe you felt in your everyday life, the less need you had for 'dangerous sports'. They hold no appeal whatsoever for Mr Phillips. You would have to see gravity as a joke or as a benign force or at the very least as something you could trifle with, play games with, not take too seriously – whereas all that Mr Phillips has to do is look downwards, at his sagged and weighted flesh, to feel differently.

The man falls with his body held in a dramatic cruciform shape, initially accelerating at thirty-two feet per second per second, beginning to slow when the band goes taut after a drop of about eighty feet, then slowing further until he comes to a momentary stop another fifty feet further down; and then the rubber coils and scrunches as the man bounces back upwards, and the cage at the end of the crane comes down to collect him. It makes Mr Phillips feel funny even to look at it. How often are there accidents? The unspoken possibility of seeing someone's death must be part of the appeal, as for the spectators at car races or air shows. A hundred thousand people go to see the British Grand Prix at Silverstone every year, paying £95 each. It's a great, though unnecessary, compliment to death.

Mr Phillips suffers from, not vertigo, but the thing that makes people unable to stand next to a height without imagining jumping or falling off it. It is as if the idea of this kind of suicide presses in on him whenever he stands in a high place. And Chelsea Bridge is the sort of elegant suspension bridge he can imagine choosing for that final jump. Why on earth would anyone throw themselves under a train when they could chuck themselves off a bridge instead?

Granted, the fall from here might not kill him, even though water is harder the faster you hit it – for some reason Mr Phillips once heard on a TV science programme but could feel himself forgetting even as he was listening to it. Say it's 100 feet up, with the tide at this lowish ebb. At 32 feet per second per second, that's $32 + (32 + 32) = 96 = 2$ seconds at a climactic speed of 64 feet per second. You multiply by 15 and divide by 22 to get miles per hour which comes to 43 miles per hour, so if it *is* true that hitting water at speed is like hitting concrete you would be hitting concrete at 43 miles per hour, which ought to do it. But there are other, more certain places. Clifton Bridge, another elegant piece of suspension work, is 250 feet which would take 4 secs, which means that you would in theory hit at $32 + 32 + 32 + 32$, which is 128 feet per second, which is 87 miles per hour, which would certainly do it. It's worth remembering that in practice you can't fall any faster than terminal velocity, which for a human being is about 130 mph which is, history shows, fast enough. Beachy Head, another popular spot, 535 feet, 5.6 seconds, close to terminal velocity. Severn Bridge, another classic, 200 feet, 3.6 seconds.

They say that you have a moment of fear and then you go all calm, or even pass out. But how on earth do they know that? And of course you would be beyond fear anyway, to do it in the first place. Otherwise the thought of your shins being driven upwards into your pelvis would put a stop to it. The moment of contact, however quick, must surely leave you with a split second of awareness of what was happening. It was like the guillotine, there had to be a fraction of a second while the head knew it was leaving the body. Even if the fall didn't kill him, the cold Thames, flowing far more powerfully and faster than anyone could swim, certainly would. Unless he went in at the turn of the tide, or landed on a boat that was carrying something soft on top or had a big canopy. What an idiot you would feel if that happened! You would have to come up with something really good to pacify the amazed bargemen. I was just looking at the paintwork and next thing I know here I am. Sorry for any alarm or inconvenience. I expect you get quite a lot of this. You couldn't drop me off at the next pier by any chance? Or, not going too far, I hope? Jolly good, I've never been to Amsterdam. They say the red light district is quite something!

Mr Phillips stands and looks down at the water for what feels like a long time.

Mr Phillips is not a well-informed bus passenger, and the only route he knows well is his standard one from Waterloo to the office. As he waits at the bus stop beside Chelsea Bridge he has no particular plans about where he wants to go. Whatever comes along first and has seating room will be fine with him. The only other aspiring passenger is a middle aged Caribbean woman in an unseasonal brown mackintosh; she looks a little like the people who come to the door in Wellesley Crescent on weekend evenings selling copies of the Jehovah's Witness newspaper. Mr Phillips thinks about getting his own reading matter out of the briefcase but before he can do anything about it a double decker bus appears.

It is one of the modern buses where you get on at the front and give your money to the driver; much slower and harder to love than the old Routemasters with the conductor. The new ones must be cheaper to run, though – less manpower. The world looks different, more fragile, when you have in mind that everyone everywhere tries to employ as few people as possible. Mr Phillips had always been impressed by the way conductors used to know exactly who had got on and off and who hadn't paid their fare, as if they had a constantly updated map of the bus in their heads. On the occasions he tried to sit still and not admit to not having paid he always found a conductor hovering at his shoulder demanding the fare. Perhaps they were trained to detect guilty body language. If a bus conductor's wife cheated on him he would know within seconds of getting home.

Mr Phillips climbs on to the step of the bus behind the supposed Jehovah's Witness. He has a good view of her big, strangely high bottom. She peremptorily flashes a bus pass at the driver. Simultaneously, as if the sight has put the thought of money in his mind, he realizes that he has no coins. His ticket from Clapham Junction to Waterloo has cleared him out of change. Mr Phillips fishes his wallet out of his jacket pocket, takes out a £10 note and says:

'I'm sorry about this.'

The driver looks at the note, where it sits in the little metal dish by his compartment.

'You're winding me up,' he says without moving. The bus thrums loudly at its standstill.

'I don't mean to. I just don't have any change,' says Mr Phillips.

'You'd like me to believe that, wouldn't you?' says the driver.

'Is my money not good enough for you?' says Mr Phillips, consciously choosing to go over to the attack.

'What was that jingling sound when you got on?' demands the driver. 'You'll tell me it's your keys. That's what you lot always say.'

'I don't have a "lot". I have ten pounds,' says Mr Phillips.

The driver looks at him without speaking for a few seconds. Then, apparently without any exertion on his part, a cascade of coins falls into a second metal dish below the first one. The driver reaches out and takes the note between thumb and first finger with an air of aggrieved delicacy. There is a chattering sound and a printed ticket extends itself from a slot.

'Eight pounds sixty change,' says the driver.

Mr Phillips takes his change and puts it into his baggy pocket – which, like everyone else's, has suffered a battering since the abolition of the pound note in favour of the chunky squid. Even if you like the pound coin, as he does, you have to admit it's hard on the old trousers. His favourite among the coin's designs is also the most common, the one with DECUS ET TUTAMEN EST cut into the rim of the coin. An ornament and a safeguard. The words are supposed to refer both to the monarchy and to the lettering itself, because it made the coins harder to forge. Mr Monroe is particularly keen on this coin. 'Amazing language, Latin,' he says. 'Just four words and it means The Holocaust Could Never Happen Here Because We've Got the Queen and Piss Off You Forgers all at the same time. I have to say that I find the Scottish motto to be in relative terms a disappointment. The design a thistle, the motto *Nemo me impune lacessit*, No One Wounds Me With Impunity. It's a prison sentiment by comparison.'

Without meeting any eyes inside the hot ground floor of the bus, Mr Phillips heads for the upper deck. As a child he loved the staircase on double decker buses. He and his parents and his sister had once stayed in a holiday cottage where the wooden spiral staircase was carved out of a ship's mast. The way the stairs twisted half-way around, like an attempt at a spiral, made him think of ships and secret passageways, shivering guards standing watches in high battlements, dragons, romance . . .

After climbing the ten feet and making two right turns Mr Phillips heads for the front of the bus, sees that there are no seats there, and then turns towards the back. It is a point of commuting and urban etiquette to take an empty double seat wherever possible rather than squeezing in beside someone already seated. Most of the passengers look as if they are on the way to work. He squeezes in beside a smartly dressed, cross-looking woman who has the air of an important person's trusted secretary.

Mr Phillips leaves his book in his briefcase. Reading it as the bus bumps and jogs would make him nauseated. Thomas has inherited this gene for motion sickness, and needs to be soothed and distracted and given breaks on journeys of any real length, whereas Martin would sit in the back happily rereading comics, and occasionally taunting his younger brother by offering to lend them to him. It is one of those issues where the difference between the two siblings seems planned and structured, as if the gene for confidence in Martin triggered the gene for shyness in Thomas, and so on with loud/quiet, liking girls' company/preferring boys', getting on better with father/mother, favourite colour purple/black, wanting a dog/wanting a cat. It was as if they took readings off each other and used them to calibrate their own whereabouts.

The bus moves half-way across Chelsea Bridge and comes to a halt. A vista opens up towards Canary Wharf in the east and past Battersea Bridge towards Hammersmith in the other direction. There isn't much traffic on the river today. There never is. Mr Phillips has lived in London his entire life and has never been afloat on the River Thames, not once. It is one of a collection of things he hasn't done. He hasn't been in a helicopter, met anyone famous, been to Wembley Stadium or the Royal Albert Hall or the House of Commons. He has never given anyone mouth-to-mouth resuscitation or made a citizen's arrest. He had never seen a dead body until his father's death in 1981. At the lying-in he was stiff and unforgettably cold to the touch.

There would be a good number of people in this town who had never ever seen a dead body – conservatively, 80 per cent. So the set of people who had never been on the Thames and had never seen a dead body would be high too. And according to the sex survey he had bought and read secretly and obsessively a couple of years before, only 30 per cent of Britons had ever experienced anal intercourse – a figure which seemed surprisingly low, for though to Mr Phillips himself the subject was neither here nor there and his own single experience, with Sharon Mitchell, had ended with her in tears and him comforting her before sneaking off to masturbate in the toilet, he knew that this was a very general number one double-top male fantasy. Indeed, the most common heterosexual male fantasy, if you ignored for the moment the one about watching women doing it with each other, was about women who were a. as keen on sex as men, if not more so, b. as quickly ready for it, c. as easily satisfied, and d. loved anal intercourse. Putting together the figures for this bus, and assuming figures of 70 per cent for no anal intercourse, 75 per cent for not having been on the Thames, 80 per cent for not having seen a dead body, and saying that there were 80 people on the bus, you multiply 70 per cent by 75 per cent by 80 per cent to get 42 per cent, which means that a total of 33.6 people on the bus have never been on London's river, seen a corpse nor experienced anal intercourse. Thanks to Sharon, Mr Phillips is in the relatively suave and experienced subset who have only not been on the Thames. He has lived.

About half the people on the bus are reading books and newspapers; the others are lost in rapt trances of pure being. They are presumably abandoned in their on-the-way-to-work thoughts, their what-I'll-say-to-him-if-he-says thoughts, their dreams of how-dare-he and how-I'll try-to-catch-her-at-the-photocopying machine, their reveries of when-I-get-home-I'll tell-him-that. As well as the usual fantasies about sex, power, recognition, revenge. A man across the bus's narrow, sticky aisle is staring into nothing while silently talking to himself. There is, if not a smile, at least a slight upward inflection at the creases of his lips. It looks as if he is rehearsing a long speech in triumphant self-justification.

Immediately beside Mr Phillips the cross-looking woman is reading a Sunday newspaper's astrology column with particularly close attention, apparently not concentrating on any one star sign but scrutinizing all of them with equal rigour. She doesn't look like a natural tabloid reader. Mr Phillips wonders if she is a sceptic checking for contradictions and internal inconsistencies, or has lots of children and close relatives and wants to monitor the auspices for all of them. Or she could be an orphan whose birth certificate had been lost and is trying to work out what month she was born in by the unscientific method of checking all horoscopes and correlating them against what happened to her, or perhaps she is simply very very interested in astrology. She notices Mr Phillips looking at her and lifts her paper slightly away from him to make his scrutiny of what she is reading more difficult. On the opposite page of her paper he catches a glimpse of a story about Clarissa Colingford, something about a secret engagement. She is known to have boyfriend trouble, multiple boyfriends, boyfriends who are caught with other women, that sort of thing. But there is no way he can find out more without actually taking the paper out of his neighbour's hands.

The bus finally gets to the end of Chelsea Bridge and begins trying to turn right. There is a small flurry of people pressing to get up, shifting their balance, setting their feet, alerting their neighbours. The more experienced commuters then wait for the bus to swing around the corner at the end of the bridge before actually standing, while neophytes bang and jostle around like pinballs as the bus lurches through its right turn. About a third of the people on the bus get off by the incinerator tower opposite Chelsea Gardens. The seat in front of Mr Phillips is now empty. For a moment he wonders if slipping into it would be an implied criticism of the other person on his double seat; then he decides that if it causes her to worry about being ugly and/or halitotic, so much the better, since she had been so sniffy about his sneaking a glimpse of her precious astrology column. Besides, she probably works for an arms dealer or some other Mr Wilkins figure or something. He moves with a fiftyish attempt at panther-like smoothness into the window seat in front. The astrology woman spreads her newspaper open across both seats with an air of complacency. A middle aged West Indian man in an enormous floppy hat comes up the stairs, followed by a schoolgirl wearing an almost parodically complete school uniform – dark grey jacket, light grey shirt, short dark blue skirt, ponytail, white socks, black shoes, satchel. They go towards the back and front of the bus respectively. The girl takes the seat right at the front with the good view but no leg room. Sticking out of the man's pocket is a battered copy of *Teach Yourself Tamil*.

Because the bus is momentarily at a halt Mr Phillips can hear the conversation of the two women in front.

'Don't know how she gets away with it,' the woman on the left, who has an Irish accent, is saying. 'If you or I did it we'd be arrested.'

'And it's not as if she's younger than us.'

'Older.'

'The trout.'

'And it's not as if it makes her look ridiculous either,' says the woman, with a note of wistfulness, before the bus roars off again and the rest of their talk is drowned out.

Mr Phillips looks at his watch, a silver-plated Omega with roman numerals which his father gave him as a present when he passed his charter exams. When Mr Phillips took the watch out of its box and looked up beaming to thank his father, the older man, with his arms crossed, merely said:

'*There*.'

At the time, that had seemed a perfectly natural thing to say; or at least Mr Phillips had felt he understood it. Now he sometimes looks at the watch and remembers his father's single word and wonders whether it meant *there*, that's the whole business of present-giving discharged – or *there*, you're a grown-up now, you need to be on time – or *there*, the days of exams are behind you – or *there,* you'll never again look at the time without remembering your father. Perhaps it really had meant, I'll be dead one day. There are times when he looks at the watch and is overcome by a recollection so acute that he can feel the stubble on his father's chin as he embraced him, and smell the slight sourness of pickled things on his breath. And at other times he just looks at his watch and thinks, Oh it's five to two.

Now, though, it's five past ten. The working day at Wilkins and Co. will be well and truly under way. When Mr Phillips was younger he had liked to be as late as was possibly consistent with keeping his job, and had been voluptuously reluctant to get out of bed. These days he likes, or liked, to be at his desk by nine fifteen, or half past at the very latest; he enjoyed setting off to work while still feeling a tad groggy, with wisps of sleep trailing behind him. There was something comforting about being seated at his desk opening his correspondence with faint vestiges of sleepiness rising off him like the steam off his day's first mug of coffee. That mug would be brought to him by Karen if she was in yet, or made by Mr Phillips himself if she had had trouble with her journey or at home. (There is a man in her life. More than that Mr Phillips does not know, and does not want to know.) Karen often looked very slightly flushed in the mornings, something to do with make-up or getting up or, perhaps, rushed sexual activity, its memory bringing a glow to her cheeks like a remembered embarrassment. And her coffee tasted better than Mr Phillips's too, which was a mystery, since it was made to precisely the same formula (two level spoonfuls of Gold Blend, water just off the boil, dollop of skimmed milk).

By half past ten Mr Phillips would hope to have read his correspondence and dictated replies to most of it. He still has his Dictaphone – it is in his briefcase at this very moment – even though it is strictly (or even not so strictly) speaking company property. But there is something so personal about this chunky piece of metal and plastic that he had felt obliged to cling on to it and to slip it home. The Dictaphone's tiny microcassette now holds replies to memos that will never be typed, signed and dispatched, letters that will never be sent, admonitions and excuses that will vanish into the electronic limbo of erased cassette tape. Mr Phillips takes the Dictaphone cassette out of his bag, holds the speaker to his ear and presses Play.

'Reply to memo from Mr Street in Administration Department,' Mr Phillips hears himself say, in the low, intimate, urgent voice he uses to his Dictaphone. 'Check to see if the early memo included a blind copy to Mr Mill and if so copy him again.'

It was Mr Mill to whom the original memo should have been sent, if he had not been so reliably inclined not to do anything about anything, ever.

'Memo begins:

'There are difficulties with the proposal to save money by switching to a cheaper brand of sticky . . . of paper with . . . er, just say Post-It notes, Karen. Full stop. To wit comma Post-It notes are patented and no cheaper brand, change that to more reasonable brand, is therefore available full stop. Apparently they were invented by an out-of-work engineer in America full stop. At the moment the budget for this item of stationery comma which costs 49p a small packet comma is fifteen thousand pounds full stop. On balance I would favour a memo from Administration informing employees of this fact comma and pointing out that free access to stationery cupboards will one day become a thing of the past if unbridled consumption of office materials cannot be checked full stop. End of memo.'

Mr Phillips stops the Dictaphone and takes it away from his

ear. It would be nice to have been the man who invented Post-It notes and to feel that your wealth was accumulating minutely but perceptibly every time someone peeled a little piece of yellow paper off a block and plunked it down on somebody else's desk. Now Wilkins and Co. would never hear of his plan to save £7500, equivalent to almost a quarter of his own annual salary, by stopping people stealing so much stuff from the office for their own use. Mr Phillips is perfectly aware that this happens since he does it himself. In the days when Mrs Phillips taught in the evenings the whole family used to communicate primarily through stolen Wilkins and Co. Post-It notes.

'The chicken is on a timer. Don't touch any of the settings. Love Mum.'

'I didn't bring you a cup of tea this morning because you looked like you needed a lie-in. We're out of bin liners.'

'Martin: the stereo in the living room was still on when I got in last night and it was hot to the touch. HOW MANY TIMES MUST I REMIND YOU TO TURN IT OFF BEFORE GO-ING TO BED.'

'Dad – five-a-side tournament moved till Sunday fortnight because of the flu epidemic can you still give me a lift Thomas.'

This might be a way of letting Mrs Phillips know what had happened.

'Darling: I'll probably be out late tonight wandering aimlessly around because I got the sack last week don't wait up love Victor.'

The enormous advantage of this method would be that he wouldn't have to be present to see her reaction, or – more probably and more painfully – her careful lack of reaction and attempt to act as if everything was OK. Knowing someone so well that you could anticipate their response to most things should make their responses easier to bear but in practice often does the opposite.

The traffic is crawling along the Embankment. Mr Phillips wants it to move more quickly, because that way there would be a greater variety of distractions. On the far side of the road, the footpath beside the river is busy with the last stray joggers of the morning, some of whom, fit scrawny men with little rucksacks, are clearly running to work. A group of twelve Gurkhas wearing olive-green T-shirts and shorts jogs past in tight formation, apparently heading for Chelsea Barracks.

About four hundred yards from Chelsea Bridge the bus stops again. There is the usual pause while people rummage for change to pay their fare and then the bus sets off. As it does so a very dishevelled man, evidently a tramp, comes to the top of the stairs. He wears a mouldy suit whose trousers are too big and whose jacket is too small, so that it seems he could burst all its seams by flexing his upper body. The trousers are kept up with knotted string. His shirt once was pink or orange. He wears shoes with the soles flapping loose and no laces, has obviously not washed or shaved for quite some time, and his face is a strange mottled purple colour. A smell of meths or turpentine seems to rise off him. He carries three very full plastic bags. He could be any age from thirty to seventy.

Mr Phillips can feel everybody on the upper deck of the bus

willing the man not to sit next to them. As if conscious of his moment in the invisible spotlight, the tramp stands at the top of the stairs and slowly scans the upper deck of the bus. Mr Phillips concentrates on avoiding eye contact while looking bored and unprovokable. The new arrival takes two steps towards the back of the bus and then with odd gracefulness swings around and heads for the front, tacking from side to side of the narrow corridor as he goes. With terrible inevitability he sways to the very front of the bus and sits down, with a loud combined sigh and cough, next to the girl in school uniform.

It isn't often, Mr Phillips thinks, that you see tramps on buses. Presumably it's the expense. On the Tube you see them all the time, especially on the Circle Line, where they got a whole day riding around and around for the price of one ticket, being spun around the capital like the flags on a prayer wheel. Mad people you saw all the time too on the Underground. In fact, after a certain time of night the Tube seemed to be populated entirely by the mad, the drunk, and the frightened.

Mr Phillips wonders what it would be like to become a tramp. If he didn't go home this evening, for instance, but simply rode the Underground until it closed, watching the ebb and flow of human types through the long day – the people travelling to work in the morning, the afternoon-shifters, the tourists with backpacks and maps and guidebooks and questions, the errand-doers, the unclassifiables on trips of all stripes, the students, hookers, nurses, actors, all those who work funny hours, then at the end of the afternoon people

94

returning from work, hanging from straps and clinging to poles in their tight hordes, heading out from the middle of town like an orderly crowd fleeing a disaster, Mr Phillips comfortably ensconced in the corner seat he has bagged during the mid-morning pre-lunch lull, in between dozes and daydreams and periods when his attention goes offline like the Wilkins and Co. IBM mainframe. Then the reverse exodus for the evening's diversions, plays and movies and pubs and clubs, and then the late-night hour of the knackered and the smashed, which leads into the slow extinction of the network, the dwindling frequencies of the trains until shutdown at one or so, when he would go to one of the big railway terminals – probably not Euston or King's Cross (too many Scotsmen, drug dealers, tarts, pimps, all that). Victoria, say, where he would try and find a spot to sleep or at least sit for the night. Later on in his career he would be more knowledgeable about soup kitchens, night shelters. He would learn the ropes.

The next day, after his first night on the skids, he would be more bedraggled, poorer – obviously there would be no getting money out of the bank without letting on where he was. And then in the days to come he would be integrated more and more completely into this new life. Becoming dog-tired on a brief excursion outside the Underground he would sit down beside a wall at the side of a pedestrian underpass, taking the weight off, and as he sat a passer-by would drop a coin in his lap, and he has become a beggar, a mendicant. Over the next days and weeks he develops his tramp routines, his pitches and places to sit; he becomes invisible, so that even if someone who knows him were to walk past – Mr Wilkins or Mr Davis-Gribben his neighbour or even Mrs Phillips – he would not be recognized. The point would be to hide in plain sight, simply to melt into the city like a raindrop in a puddle. It would be a version of what men in India did, making their pile and providing for their families before going off to be a *sanyassin*, a holy man, free of earthly connections; free of family. To live without love, that would be the idea.

The tramp at the front of the bus seems to be attempting to start a conversation with the schoolgirl. At least he is making noises in her direction while she looks out of the window trying to ignore him, the poor thing. It's such a feature of city life, being bearded by madmen and weirdoes. When Thomas played in the all-conquering St Winifred's Under-11 football team their matches attracted a regular spectator who wore a green duffle coat and a matching felt hat decorated with three prominent feathers. These were different each week, and looked as if they had been freshly plucked. The man was always either beaming as if he had just won the Pools or scowling like a mad vicar about to launch into a sermon denouncing everything he saw. No one knew who he was. When Eric Harris, father of Wayne, the team's little right-footed left back, approached him he would only say, 'There's not much I can admit to. I'm scouting for one of the big clubs, the very big clubs.'

'Nutter' was Eric's summing up.

'But is he dangerous?' asked Mr Slocombe, whose son Grant wore glasses and was the team's controversial goal-keeper – a good shot-stopper but weak on crosses.

Mr Harris thought about that while the two teams ran around the field being shouted at by their fathers.

'Nah.'

This verdict proved true. The man had come to every match for a whole season and was then never seen again. By the end of that time Mr Phillips came to feel that, compared to many of the fathers, screaming orders at their boys to make ever greater and more violent effort, the poor madman's presence was oddly soothing.

The schoolgirl in the front seat seems to be reaching a similar verdict about the tramp sitting next to her. He has said something to her that made her laugh, and she is now chatting to him, apparently happily. In fact she is smiling and giggling as he speaks. It is easy to see that if you were a funny tramp, that would give you an advantage over other tramps, Mr Phillips could recognize that. Humour is a help in almost any walk of life.

Mr Phillips has been on board the bus for about half an hour. In that time they have travelled roughly a thousand yards. His body feels as if it is secreting packets of heat about itself; when he shifts in his seat a moist, intimate gust of ball-sweat wafts up to his nostrils. But after having been completely immobile for several minutes, the bus finally squeezes over into the right-hand lane and chugs past the obstacle that has been blocking traffic. This is a huge hole in the ground, surrounded by plastic sheeting, out of which water is boiling on to the surface of the road. A group of workmen stands around the hole in bright orange safety vests and helmets. Burst water main? It is probably something to do with those miles and miles of stinking, crumbling, brick-lined Victorian sewers, each awash with everything from sink slops to rainfall run-off to plastic bags, tampons, pet frogs, coagulating kitchen fat, all the stuff people flush and wash away, not of course forgetting every imaginable variety of urine and excrement. The mad Religious Education teacher at school, Mr Erith, whose pupils would often sit listening half aghast and half trying not to giggle as he ranted on about his favourite subject, sin (he was the only teacher in the history of teaching for whom the word *sin* was a sure-fire, guaranteed successful red herring, leading to a forty-minute speech on the subject) – Mr Erith had liked to quote to his blushing and sniggering charges St Augustine's words that we are born *inter urinam et faeces*.

'Don't be deceived into thinking that these are technical terms,' Mr Erith had added, his height and width and not-quite-clerical black suit adding to both the comedy and the menace he always projected. There were rumours of the usual lurid schoolboy sort around Mr Erith, and they all contained this combination of the ridiculous and the sinister. He had been an Army chaplain who was kicked out after going on the rampage and killing an enormous number of Germans, rending them limb from limb with his bare hands. (Mr Phillips had done the sums and this didn't quite work – Mr Erith, in his mid thirties during the late fifties, would have had to have been one of the British Army's rare teenage padres.) He had been an Olympic level discus thrower who gave up athletics for God before being given up by God in his turn and leaving the seminary to become a teacher. He had been kicked out of priest's school for holding seances. He had been kicked out for beating up another seminarian, after an argument about theology and/or women. He had been kicked out for beating up the college principal, who had rigged the exams so that he failed because the principal had worked out that he was having an affair with his wife. Those were the sorts of rumour.

'*Urinam et faeces* – this is demotic language. "Piss" and "shit". Todhunter, did you have something you wanted to share with us?'

An involuntary squeak had come out of Todhunter, who was a known giggler.

'No sir.'

Mr Erith gave one of his rare, disconcerting smiles. His bared teeth were a rich yellow, the colour of mature ivory.

'Good. *Inter urinam et faeces* – and that is how we live, too, above a rotting superstructure of sewage and effluent. Think of how much hideous waste is evacuated from this very school building every day. The pipes creaking and straining with it. The plumbing stretched to full capacity to deal with your unspeakable effluvia. Then multiply that by the number of similar buildings in London. Then add the private homes, the public so-called conveniences, the gutters and urinals and all the other subterranean conduits of Augustine's two substances, whose names I shall not speak again since Todhunter seems unable to contain his amusement at the sound of them. And then with this image fresh in your minds understand that you have something not even a thousandth, not a hundred thousandth or a millionth, as repulsive as what God sees when he looks at us and he sees our –'

At this point Mr Erith thumped his heavy fist on the desk, so that its jars of pencils and chalks hopped into the air, and he raised his voice to a hoarse bark:

'– SIN.'

He was breathing hard. The result of this speech was that Mr Phillips thought of his old RE teacher every time the subject of London's sewers came to his mind. 'London's crumbling Victorian sewers' was what they were always called.

The tramp at the front of the bus must be, has to be, certainly looks, very smelly. He has the ingrained patina of dirt which comes from living rough. Not that this seems to put the schoolgirl off, and the two of them now appear to be getting on famously. Almost everything the tramp says seems to reduce her to helpless laughter. In turn, when she speaks he leans forward 'hanging on her every word'. 'If you can make them laugh you're half-way there,' Mr Phillips once heard girl-confident Martin confiding to girl-shy Thomas in the back of the car on the way home from a party. The tramp seems to be acting on the same maxim. His armpits and sweat-steeped clothes must be emitting who knows what odours; but she doesn't seem to mind in the least. In fact, convulsing with laughter at this latest sally, she leans forward and slaps him on the thigh as if begging him to stop before she breaks a rib. It is an unschoolgirlish gesture and an unexpected one, though not as unexpected as what follows as the tramp, seizing the day, kisses her on the side of her cheek as she turns away.

Sweet sixteen and never been kissed, thinks Mr Phillips, not very relevantly, but then he feels his grip on things beginning to loosen. Now she is looking down, blushing, but not seeming too unhappy about the latest development. The same could not be said for the rest of the passengers on the upper deck. There are mutterings and rufflings, muffled consternation. The two women in front of Mr Phillips are whispering unoverhearable shocked somethings to each other. Then they go silent and rigid as the tramp reaches out, oddly gentle, and turns the girl's face towards him and starts kissing her in earnest. A voice from towards the back of the bus, audibly anguished, gives an involuntary cry of 'No!' Someone else can be heard to say, 'Somebody stop him!' But the person most closely concerned, the schoolgirl herself, evidently doesn't want to stop him. She is energetically returning the tramp's kisses; from the way their cheeks and jaws are moving you can clearly tell that both sets of tongues are involved. Mr Phillips feels the twinge of nausea that always overtakes him when he sees people kissing – actors on the screen are bad enough, real

101

people are always worse. It is something to do with the texture of tongues, their snail-like smoothness and sliminess, and the idea of other people's mouths; you wouldn't want to explore someone else's mouth in theory, only in practice. At Grimshaw's the most junior accountants had a popular game called Would You Rather, involving the invention of fantastically repulsive alternatives: 'Would you rather' – a voice would ask, usually in the pub after work – 'suck snot off Mr Wink's moustache or have poxy Patty (the boss's twenty-stone secretary) sit on your face and fart?' For Mr Phillips, keen on kissing in practice, the idea of kissing has something of a 'would you rather' about it.

These two have no such difficulty. The tramp and the schoolgirl are now openly engaged in what can only be described as a snog. One of his hands is clamped to the back of her head. The other is out of sight elsewhere about her person. Her eyes are closed, her arms around him. Luckily the bus is making too much noise for any cries or moans to be audible. Mr Phillips doesn't know what to think. He is looking straight ahead, slightly to one side of the couple, but they are on full display in his peripheral vision.

'Ought to be a law against it,' he catches from one of the women in front of him. She is in an ecstasy of outraged propriety.

The bus stops. They are further along the Embankment, just to the south of Victoria Station. The tramp and the schoolgirl seem to have reached some agreement. They get up together, tittering happily and leaning against each other, and make for the stairs, which the girl descends first, her hand stretched back to the tramp, who looks younger and happier than he did when he got on but still far gone in filth. There is a general sense of relief in which Mr Phillips shares. Mr Phillips hears someone say the actual words 'Well I never'. He risks a look out of the window at the happy couple who are now sort of skipping off up the pavement.

Mr Phillips himself gets off the bus two stops later. The traffic is still crawling and he feels the need to travel at a more human pace. A group of other passengers seem to have made the same choice and decant themselves on to the streets carrying briefcases, bags, newspapers, jackets. Quite large numbers of people are moving along the pavement in the same direction that the bus was travelling. Many of them are tourists. Further up the street, coaches are disgorging their passengers and taxis are dropping people off; in short, a maelstrom of people and vehicles. Mr Phillips realizes that he is standing just down the road from the Tate Gallery. In fact, looking up the Embankment he can see that an orderly queue has formed, three across and a hundred or so yards long, heading towards a tent-like structure beside the gallery's main building. Above that there is a sign advertising an exhibition called *Manet*, along with dates, times and prices.

It is odd to see so many people happily carrying brightly coloured rucksacks as if they were badges of liberation and the ability to go anywhere, do anything, have no constraints. For anyone roughly Mr Phillips's age, rucksacks are heavy, sodden canvas objects associated with being in the Army and with the specific absence of liberty and of being able to do what you liked. Even at St Aloysius's, which had less of all that than many schools, rucksacks were still associated with extreme boredom and fatigue. (Mr Phillips had joined the cadets and turned out to be good at drill, the best in his year group. All you had to do was what you were told.)

One tall boy in the queue has a tiny pink rucksack with yellow straps and fittings with the word 'Sexy' picked out in lime-green sequins. His hair is shaved at the sides and he wears a T-shirt with capped sleeves. He looks very fit, at least as fit as Mr Phillips had been at the end of his school days, when he had been fitter than at any other point in his life. Walking past the queue is a girl from the lower deck of the bus. She is wearing the shortest skirt Mr Phillips has ever seen; so short that the lower part of her buttocks are visible at the top of her thighs. The flesh there is slightly mottled, not quite with nodules of cellulite – she's too young for that – but with a curious pale, corrugated texture like that of chicken skin. She also wears clogs and a pink T-shirt. Her brown hair is cut so short that her top vertebrae have a knobbly prominence. Her appearance gives Mr Phillips a pang of envy that girls in his day had not dressed like that and a near-simultaneous twinge of relief, since if they had he would never have summed up the courage to talk to them. She does not so much walk off as totter, making one or two smoothing-down gestures at her skirt, about which she seems with some justification to be a little self-conscious. Perhaps she has grown taller since the last time she wore it. Certainly it is well within the category of what Martin would call a 'pussy pelmet'.

'Clothes are a sign of the Fall not because they conceal our God-created nakedness but because they provoke desire,' says a Caribbean woman's voice immediately behind Mr Phillips's right ear. He turns around. It is the Jehovah's Witness, who has been watching him watch the girl and is now looking at him with real hostility.

'Sorry,' says Mr Phillips.

Most of the younger people seem to have arrived independently, on foot and via public transport. Older people come in coach parties. A seventyish couple, looking very thoroughly used to each other, are leaning together puffing as they recover from having climbed down the steps of their coach. On the steps outside the front of the museum several dozen younger people, foreign-looking (darker skin, different clothes), are sitting chatting, gossiping, smoking, picking each other up, looking at guidebooks and what's-on magazines, eating crisps and sandwiches and drinking soft drinks, or just staring into space. One girl, whose bobbed black hair circles down at the corners of her face as if putting her expression in brackets, is methodically blowing bubble gum. Mr Phillips remembers that feeling of waiting for something to happen, so strong when we're young and so hard to recapture afterwards, just as boredom could be like a physical pain while it was happening but was impossible to recover through memory.

Many of the people sitting on the stairs look little more than children. They are certainly a lot younger than Mr Phillips had been before he had any comparable freedom. When Martin went off on his first holiday with friends, at the age of seventeen, Mr Phillips had felt a stab of fear and pity for his youth and vulnerability. Two years (it felt like two minutes) later he was Railcarding around Europe on his own, getting up to who knew what who knew where with who knew whom. It was a hard time for Mr and Mrs Phillips, who had had their patience tested to destruction during Martin's teenage years. These began late – he had been easygoing and affable right up until he turned fifteen – and then made up for it with the intensity of his fuckedoffness. The anxiety they felt when he travelled was a half-welcome reminder that they did, in fact, after all, love him. Mr Phillips had noticed at the time that as children we all occasionally wish or fantasize that our parents were dead – but the reverse doesn't apply.

Martin's six-week trip yielded them four postcards, each of which brought with it a specific and vivid set of worrying images (Amsterdam: drugs! Copenhagen: Aids! Berlin: skinheads! Athens: pollution!), and a single telephone call, from a village in Greece where the only payphone was broken, enabling people to call anywhere in the world for free. He came back with a short and neat beard that had unexpected red bits at the corners of his mouth. That and his eerily deep tan made him look a good five years older. After that trip he was never quite as angry, or as dismissive, or as sullen, or as close to them; it was when he began to leave home. Mr Phillips can't help wondering what's in store for the parents of all these children. Somewhere each of them has someone worrying themselves sick.

As in a film or an advertisement, a boy travelling at speed hurtles up the steps past Mr Phillips and down on to the step beside the girl with the Louise Brooks bob and begins kissing her energetically. Mr Phillips has to look away before he finds out what happens to the bubble gum.

For a moment Mr Phillips thinks about queuing for the big exhibition. But long queues, which are always the closest imaginable thing to being dead, are probably not a good idea today. So instead he weaves up the steps and through the revolving doors, behind a waddling man in trainers and a sun-hat whose enormous jeans are hitched up to his sternum, and goes into the main gallery.

It is immediately cooler and more noisy than the city outside. Some people are standing in front of the table where bags are being, not very convincingly, searched by a pair of guards in amateurish uniforms which look as if they had been made on a sewing machine at home. This will be all about bombs, presumably, one of those London things you get used to, unless it was also to scan for nutters who wanted to carve paintings up with Stanley knives or spray paint on them or set light to them or whatever. Chop them up with a machete until cornered by the underpaid, half-asleep guards. I'll take two of you with me!

Mr Phillips goes over to the searchers. In a gesture that feels vaguely sexual, he opens his briefcase and invites them to rummage in it. One of the guards looks and languidly moves a manila folder out of the way with a gloved hand. The folder contains a thick pad of the A4 graph paper ruled into 1 mm squares that Mr Phillips likes to use for taking notes and calculations. This particular pad contains the left-over sums for the Post-It Note memo, and a first draft of some sums he made about his and Mrs Phillips's financial position when he had first heard that he had been made redundant. The other objects in the briefcase are: a calculator; a plastic ruler; a plastic box – a 'pocket protector' – with two HB pencils, a sharpener, a Rotring fine-nibbed technical drawing pen, and two black Bic biros; his Wilkins and Co. desk diary, which he has taken from his office and forgotten to remove from his briefcase; a spare tie with yellow and green horizontal stripes, a Christmas present from Thomas three years ago, ditto; a Wilkins and Co. pocket diary; an empty hip flask that Mrs Phillips gave him for emergencies, which he keeps in the briefcase for sentimental reasons only, since when it was full it leaked and made his papers smell of whisky; his office toothbrush, which has a useful little cap to stop it smearing paste everywhere; Bobby Moore's autobiography; a silver-plated letter opener that he inherited from his father and which he, like his father, never uses; a small packet of tissues; his copy of the *Daily Mail*; two packets of Post-It notes.

The guard looks at all this without any sign of curiosity or recognition. He nods at Mr Phillips, who takes that as a sign to close the briefcase.

Mr Phillips walks into the first rotunda inside the gallery and takes a floor plan out of the plastic holder. Then he decides he would prefer to wander aimlessly around and puts the map back; it doesn't seem right to take something for nothing, especially if he isn't going to put the something to any use. Anyone who has any memory at all of the forties in Britain has a different attitude towards waste than anyone who doesn't. Mr Phillips was nine when rationing ended and can still remember the atmosphere of straitenedness and not quite privation. It is odd to think that he has only moved about three miles from where he lived then, in a middle-of-terrace house with his parents and his two-years-older sister. Because films of the period were always in black and white it sometimes seems that his memories are black and white too, especially his only real war memory, which has to do with the bomb damage that took years to repair. They were far enough from the docks to have been spared a lot of it, but Mr Phillips feels as if he can still remember – it is on the cusp between a real memory and something he has been told about so often he can see it – the way some homes had been turned inside out, excavated or split open like dolls' houses, so that you could see a mirror askew with its glass shattered but its gilt frame intact still hanging in an upstairs bedroom, with the rest of the floor melting downwards and outwards like a partially eaten gingerbread house; or the way the ruined kitchen was open to full view; or the beams and pipings which made it look as if the house were spilling its guts. All the inhabitants had died, some of the 30,000 Londoners who died in the bombing. This is a number about which he sometimes thinks, and compares with other numbers when they come in books or TV programmes or newspaper articles. It could be expressed mathematically: 30,000 (Londoners killed in the blitz) < 42,000 (Germans killed in Hamburg fire storm) > 32,000 (number of U-boat sailors who died) < 2,800,000 (Russian POWs who died in German prison camps) > 78,000 (Japanese killed in the bombing of Hiroshima) < 2,200,000 (Chinese who died during the Japanese invasion) > 90,000 (Americans who died in the war in the Pacific) < 395,000 (British and Commonwealth dead in the war) < 1,000,000 (British and Commonwealth dead in World War One) > 60,000 (British dead on first day of the Somme) > 26,000 (US dead in battle of Guadalcanal) < 30,000 (American airmen based in East Anglia killed in daylight bombing raids on Germany) = number killed in London in the Blitz. The thing was that about half-way through doing the sums you went sort of numb and the numbers ceased to be anything other than numbers, as also happened when dealing with sums of money not your own, even if you were a trained accountant.

Another memory of the forties was the taste of coffee. In 1949 his father had arrived home with a tiny sachet of real coffee twisted in a piece of brown wrapping paper. It was a gift from some bigwig who had been done a personal favour by his boss. That same evening Mr Phillips's father carefully supervised his wife as she made a pot of coffee, standing fussily over the stove with something maternal in his solicitude for the ground brown beans. When the coffee was made his parents sat sipping it out of their best cups, not talking.

'Would you like a taste?' his father asked. Mr Phillips had been too shy to ask; except of course that standing by the kitchen table softly panting was in itself a way of asking. He nodded and his father passed to him the thin blue and white china cup. With both hands around it, Mr Phillips took a careful sip, and at the same time caught his first noseful of the acrid, hot aroma. Luckily he did not gasp or spit but handed the cup back to his father without mishap.

'Well?' his father asked. Mr Phillips was at a loss for words. He said:

'Thank you, papa.'

His father smiled and returned to his communion with the cup.

'It's really for grown-ups,' he said. There is still a certain coffee taste – the bottom of the mug in a colleague's office, or a really nasty after-dinner cup in a friend's house – which transports him as if physically back to their kitchen in Wandsworth in 1949, when the thin, acrid, bitter, watery taste had been the rarest and most precious thing in the world.

2.4

Mr Phillips moves past a couple who have positioned themselves almost blocking the entrance to the main gallery, each
holding one end of a folded-out plan, like scheming generals.
They are in comfortable, spreading middle age – the man's
shoulders, waist and hips slide downwards into each other as
easily as Mr Phillips's own – but are dressed like students in
jeans and clumpy trainers.

'I dunno,' says the man. His accent is American but once
had not been; he is from somewhere else, Ulster or Scotland
perhaps. Hybridized accents are harder to unpick than neat
ones, even for the English, every single one of whom has a top-
of-the-range on-board computer calculating the exact geo-
graphical and social location of the speaker every time
somebody opens his mouth. Grammar school-educated Mr
Phillips's accent is Received Pronunciation overlying a stra-
tum of South London. Martin and Tom both speak with a mild
South London rasp that they can, especially Martin, roughen
up or tone down at will. Mrs Phillips speaks a beautifully neutral form of RP that Mr Phillips had once found sexy – it was
part of the idea of having sex with someone posher than you
were. Class makes sex more interesting for everybody. Karen's
accent, East London verging on Essex, is sexy too, but in a

more straightforwardly sluttish way. And there is something about the limitless reserves of indifference she can express, the thrilling estuarine boredness of her 'Yeah'.

The woman holding the map with the mystery-accent man is wearing jeans that reveal her waist size to be 36 and her inner leg to be 30. Truth in advertising.

'The Pre-Raphaelites just don't do it for me,' she says.

'They were fags,' says the man.

'Ruskin was definitely a fag.'

'Watts sure paints like one.'

That seems to cover the subject.

Mr Phillips heads into a long narrow room with sculptures that runs down the centre of the building. As always when he goes to a museum his impetus runs out very quickly once he has got inside. He has a feeling that he is looking for something that is not there, and what is worse, that everyone else is too. Or that they know something which he doesn't. Or that there are a set of feelings he is supposed to have in the presence of art but which in his case are simply absent. If he is honest with himself he would rather have been looking at photographs of naked women. If he is to look at things he would rather look at things that are forbidden.

Mr Phillips stands in front of a sculpted head by someone called Henri Gaudier-Brzeska. The head is two different heads melted into one, or has two very different halves, with one eye higher than the other and a nose that points off to the left as you look at it. At the same time it has a streamlined quality. Also there is something Polynesian about it. Like all those modern things with different bits and projections it implies that people are different at different times and contain lots of aspects to themselves. We are all many. Seven out of ten.

Mr Phillips stands in front of *Ophelia* by Millais. She is lying there waiting to drown. Mr Phillips has never seen a dead woman. The field was limited: his grandmother had had a closed coffin and in any case he had only been seven years old. Mr Phillips's mother went to live in Australia with his sister when his father died in 1981. When she dies he will go to the funeral; this grieving twenty-four hour plane trip, the longest and worst journey he will ever make, looms somewhere in the future.

Unless it is a side-effect of hearing the couple under the rotunda, this is one of the paintings that make you wonder about the sexual life of the painter. Had he liked the idea of doing it with a dead girl? Some men did. At his first employer, Grimshaw's, Mr Phillips knew a man called Smilt whose sister had told him that her husband liked her to have a very cold bath before coming to bed and then lying absolutely still. What made it worse was that the man was an undertaker. Mr Phillips had filed that one under 'It takes all sorts.'

Also, this painter obviously had a thing about hair. And people who had a thing about hair were supposed to be masochists. Or was that people who had a thing about feet? But that went oddly with liking dead girls; surely you couldn't like the idea of having pain inflicted on you by a dead girl? No. And then there was the redhead aspect. This was a whole subject in itself. Mr Phillips had never been to bed with a redheaded girl and felt envious of anyone who had. But when you thought about it, Millais might well not be in that category.

Also, if she was mad surely she wouldn't be calmly floating on her back like that? Six out of ten.

Mr Phillips stands in front of *The Boyhood of Raleigh*. A colourfully dressed man is sitting talking to two boys. He has an earring and a headkerchief. Nowadays this scene would probably be reported to the police and you could be fairly sure he was a pervert. Mr Phillips has virtually a whole album full of photographs which would now stand a decent chance of getting him and Mrs Phillips arrested, some busybody at Boots tipping off the police to raid them and take away pictures of Martin and Tom in various states of undress, in the bath, in bed, asleep and so on. It has to be admitted that the pirate-type man bullshitting away to the little boys does not look the opposite of a paedophile; there certainly is something over-eager about him, and if he does like little boys, the young Raleigh's adorable frilly collar would presumably be like a ham sandwich spreading itself with mustard and lying down in front of a hungry man with a cry of 'Eat me, eat me!' And then of course sailors were notoriously keen on all that. Plus the idea of the picture was so stupid, as if you ended up doing what you did because someone had told you yarns as a child – as if his father had spun tales about the glamour and wonder of accounting, or he had dandled Martin on his knees and kept him spellbound by recounting the glorious annals of the recording industry. Five out of ten.

Mr Phillips stands in front of *The Fairy Feller's Master Stroke* by Richard Dadd. This is a picture he has been to look at on each of the four occasions he has gone to look around the Tate (early date with Mrs Phillips, when he was trying to seem cultured; two visits with his sister and her daughters when they came to London and were doing the sights; and this one). This is on the borderline for disqualification from being a true Londoner, since as all Londoners know, real Londoners never go to do or see anything in their own city. The exception is those unfortunates with small children, forever having to go to circuses and cartoons and pantomimes and adventure playgrounds and rare breed parks. But that doesn't really count. In his fifty years in the city Mr Phillips has been to the Tower of London once, on a school trip; the British Museum twice, once on a school trip and once with his nieces while his sister and Mrs Phillips went shopping; Madame Tussaud's once, with Martin and Thomas; once to the National Gallery for the same reason; once to the National Theatre with Martin; and that was more or less it, so that he had never once been to Kew Gardens or Hampton Court or the naval museum at Greenwich or Teddington Lock or the Royal Opera House or the Barbican or the Trooping of the Colour or the Changing of the Guards or the Last Night of the Proms or indeed the Proms (Mrs Phillips went enough for both of them) or the Motor Show or the Planetarium or the annual open day in Highgate Cemetery. Excluding annual visits to the Richmond pantomime between 1977 (after Martin's sixth birthday) and 1989 (Tom's tenth) he has been to the theatre five times, which is five times more than he would have gone if it had been left entirely to him.

In the old days one of the London activities Mr Phillips would probably have not done was go and look at the inhabitants of Bedlam on a Sunday afternoon. He knew about this because the first time he had been to the Tate a man with a posh voice was leading a party around and they had stood in front of *The Fairy Feller's Master Stroke* while Mr Phillips hung on the edge of earshot. The man who painted it had killed his father with an axe. He was called Richard Dadd, which was quite funny. He spent the rest of his life in the main loony bin, which for some reason was called Bethlehem (hence Bedlam). Mad Dadd killed his bad dad.

'The elements of dementia in Dadd's vision', said the posh man, 'speak for themselves.' Every time he sees this picture Mr Phillips wonders what that meant. In his view either everything spoke for itself or nothing did. But the painting is small and very energetic and full of elves and goblins and things. Perhaps Dadd had thought he was the fairy feller himself, when he brought the axe down on his father's head? It wasn't the sort of thing you could do if you were aware of what you were doing. Eight out of ten, thinks Mr Phillips.

Mr Phillips stands in front of a double portrait by Stanley Spencer. It is a picture of the artist and his wife lying side by

side with no clothes on in a room that looks untidy and probably cold. The woman has red hair and one of those cross redhead's faces. Her breasts have curious tinges of green in them.
If that was what naked women usually looked like pornography would never have caught on. The man looks like a swot
but also randy and quite nice – you are on his side. At the foot
of the painting lies a strangely expressive leg of mutton (Mr
Phillips's favourite meat) dressed for the oven.

Spencer has painted his own penis with lavish and loving
care. It is quite big, too. Mr Phillips thinks about this for a
moment. If you looked down at it it was supposed to be fore-
shortened, but of course you could always hold it out in front
of you and/or use a ruler. Or you could position yourself in
front of a mirror which is perhaps what Sir Stanley had done.
If the mirror was leaning backwards slightly so that you could
look down on it, and it was resting on the floor or at least
below waist height, then it would certainly make it look bigger. That was elementary perspective. Plus it was towards the
front of the picture and made to look bigger that way too. Of
course if you were going to paint your own cock you would
take steps to make it show to advantage. It stood to reason.
Nine out of ten, Mr Phillips is thinking, as a woman's voice
behind him says,

'Yes yes yes yes yes yes yes.'

Mr Phillips turns around. A woman in a red coat and
matching but very eccentric sort-of-beret is looking at the
painting and nodding her head. One or two other people shift

to other parts of the room as if, like dogs reacting to an ultra-sonic whistle, they are responding to the way the woman's madness is broadcasting on an extra-sensory frequency. Before Mr Phillips can look away she makes eye contact.

'They didn't used to do it, you know. It wasn't that he couldn't manage it. She wouldn't let him.'

'Do what?'

'It – you know. Sex. He was a Christian, he was horny as a toad, and they never did it. You can see it in the picture if you look closely enough.'

Mr Phillips looks at the picture again. He has to admit that he can't see it, unless it is in the fact that you wouldn't bother painting yourself about-to-do-it or just-having-done-it when you could use the same energy to do it instead. Perhaps that is why double nude self-portraits are rare. The woman comes up beside Mr Phillips and says:

'Brrrrrrr.' Then, turning to him with a surprisingly sweet, sane smile she says, 'It's such a cold picture.'

Mr Phillips smiles politely and noncommittally back. He moves towards the Clore gallery where the Turners hang and then, like a man shaking off a tail in a thriller, dodges left towards British Surrealism 1900–1966. The woman unembarrassedly doubles back after him. He realizes that he has been adopted.

'I've not seen you here before,' she says as they stand in front of a John Craxton painting which features multicoloured cubist goats. 'You're not one of the regulars.'

'Would you expect to know me if I was a regular?' asks Mr Phillips.

'Heavens yes,' says the woman. 'I come here every day. Mainly I come to heckle the tour guides. They talk the most fearful tripe and need much correcting. I used to pick them up on more or less everything they said but now I wait for errors of fact before I pounce. I think it helps them keep on their toes. Then once I've established a bridgehead I broaden out into more general interpretative points. I like to think that my perspective is broadly feminist though also unmistakably personal. And then sometimes, not often but every now and then, I like to spout any old mad rubbish just to see if they notice the difference and you know the shocking thing is they never seem to.'

'Yes, that is disturbing', says Mr Phillips.

'This building used to be a prison, you know,' the woman goes on as they walk further into the Surrealism room. 'That's why there are so few doors. You want to stop people getting in and out too easily. Just as you can't walk in and out of a prison so you can't walk in and out of an art gallery. Do you ever wonder why, of all the epochs of the world, now should be the most populous? Why so many souls should have chosen now of all times to be born?'

'No.'

'Nor do I. It seems perfectly obvious to me.'

They stopped as if by mutual consent in front of a painting of a man eating something, like a Dalí only even worse. Four out of ten.

'It ought really to be like it was in the war,' says the woman. 'The National Gallery was sent into hiding and only one picture was taken out and put on show at any one time. The longing for art! The concentration, the hunger, with which people yearned for it! A great city should have no more than one picture on display. Let it change once a week, once a month. We would recapture our seriousness! The jewel in our crown!'

'Does it matter?' asks Mr Phillips.

'Heavens yes. Why do you think all these people are here? What sort of behaviour do you think you are observing?'

Mr Phillips is thinking about that in a desultory way when with a surge of horror he sees, coming into the room from the opposite end, Mrs Palmer, wife to Mr Palmer, a.k.a. Norman the Noxious Neighbour. Mr Phillips can vaguely remember hearing something about an Open University course – it must be to do with that. At the moment she is looking down at a gallery plan but she is only about fifteen feet away and can't fail to notice Mr Phillips when she looks up. That will lead her to start talking to him, which will make him have to explain what he is doing in the Tate Gallery at eleven o'clock on a Monday morning. She will then go home and ask her husband to guess who she bumped into and Mr Phillips's quality of life at Wellesley Crescent will take a significant turn for the worse. He abruptly turns and heads back the way he came.

'Aren't we a wriggly one!' says the woman, still at his heels. 'But I'm not so easily left behind as all that!'

Mr Phillips feels a wave of tremendous fatigue, of a sort he doesn't remember experiencing since the last time he was in the same building five years before. What is it about looking at pictures that makes you feel so knackered?

'I think I've had enough,' he says. 'I don't have much stamina for this sort of thing.'

'Quite so. You're very sensible. It is the emanations of spirit coming off the paintings which is so exhausting. The vibrations they might once have been called. If one thinks of it as spiritual exercise which drains and refreshes in the same way that physical exercise drains and refreshes, does that make it feel any better? No. Of course not.' Another sweet, sane smile.

A tour party comes out of the next gallery at the end of the room, the man at the head of the party looking shifty as he walks past Mr Phillips and his new chum. Mr Phillips wonders if it is the same man with the posh voice who thought that the signs of dementia spoke for themselves. A light enters the woman's eyes and she peels off to follow the group, squeezing Mr Phillips's arm in abrupt farewell as she leaves.

Outside the gallery Mr Phillips takes a couple of lungfuls of London air at the top of the steps. The sky is now clear and blue, and it is hot. Beside him stands a girl with black sandals and red feet.

'You have time?' she says in a Spanish or Portuguese accent. A voice in Mr Phillips's head says If you've got the inclination and If you've got the money and You interest me strangely and But this is so sudden. The voice that comes out of his mouth says:

'Five past eleven.' The girl nods and bites her lip.

Mr Phillips goes down to the Embankment and turns left towards Westminster. Across the Thames the sun is bright on the huge colourful building, all trees and ziggurats and pyramids and long glass windows, that houses the Secret Service. As always when he passes the building Mr Phillips stops for a look. You never see anyone moving about inside it, or going into it from the street in Vauxhall, so clever things have obviously been done with the doors and windows. At the same time there is something odd about spies going to work in a brand-new office building that is one of the most conspicuous and extrovert and obviously expensive in the whole of London.

It would be good fun to be a spy, and never to be allowed to tell anyone what you did. Not even Mrs Phillips, except in the most general terms. Certainly not Martin or Thomas. As for the neighbours, they would only know that you were something in the civil service, probably to do with fish quotas or harmonising EU policy in relation to tractor parts. And all the time you were standing at a barbecue while the man on your right boasted about his new Rover 816 and the man on your left talked about the council's inability to empty the bins without leaving more mess strewn all over the road behind them than there was before they started, you would be thinking about whatever it was that spies thought about, and the main thing would be that nobody would have the faintest idea what was on your mind. And when Mrs Phillips says something like 'What are you thinking?' or 'A penny for them?' you wouldn't be able to tell her, by law. You wouldn't be able to say, 'I'm worried about the quality of information we're getting back from our network in Tripoli via his dead letter microdot burst transmission' – you would have to say instead, 'I was wondering whether after all we should have pushed Tom to keep up with his piano lessons' or 'Just trying to remember where I left the remote control, darling.'

The traffic has improved very slightly and Mr Phillips doesn't feel as if the air is quite so edible with impurities. He heads along the Embankment towards Westminster. A walk: that is the idea. It has been years since he travelled around central London on foot – literally years, not since his bachelor days when he had lived in Shepherd's Bush and would often travel into the West End to meet friends and go to the pub or whatever. It goes without saying that not walking is one reason he is now so fat; driving, like marriage, makes men fat.

The only pedestrians in this part of town at this time of day are occasional stray tourists. All the office workers have arrived at the office and are happily or unhappily immersed in their days. At about this point on a normal day Mr Phillips would be in a meeting, since eleven o'clock conferences were a regular feature at Wilkins and Co. Today being the last Monday in the month he would normally expect to be in a budget meeting with the planning department, which essentially involved sitting there listening to them drone on before he and his colleagues could take away the figures and shoot lots of holes in them. This could be done at the meeting, but Mr Phillips preferred to do it by memo since he didn't have much appetite for the confrontation involved – which would often be considerable, since the planning department was strikingly, remarkably, bad at sums. Their projected cost for insulating the offices at the company's main plant in Banbury had once been wrong by 173 per cent.

When he was younger Mr Phillips had hated meetings. Or at least he had once he had got over the grown-up feeling, the warm glow of inclusion, of being invited to his first meeting with his first employers, Grimshaw's. Children and students didn't have meetings; only adults, serious employed people had them. So at the start there was the sense of being a big boy now. But Mr Phillips soon came to dread the whole business of sitting around a table with colleagues pretending to decide things. He hated the rooms in which meetings took place, with their horrible large tables and nasty chairs, with arms for the important people at the ends of the room, and the dank smell of the company coffee on the hotplate, and people's briefcases, calculators, pencils, notebooks, agendas, personal organizers, beepers, copies of last meeting's minutes, all of it. Most of all he hated the feeling that they were all impostors or impersonators, and with it the feeling that they were conspiring together to kill time, so that every second in the meeting was being wilfully murdered, bludgeoned to death. At other times he felt that it was more casual, as if the time was just being pissed away, the way you might piss away hours in the pub or by watching bad TV, or Martin and Tom would by playing a computer game.

It would be possible to calculate how much time in the course of a life was spent not doing anything. Obviously sleep was controversial in this context, since you could count that as either doing something or not. For Mr Phillips it is very much an activity, and an important one. So excluding that, Mr Phillips reckoned that he had spent, not doing anything:

– as a child before school age: six hours a day, conservatively, excluding time spent being fed, taught to read etc., time playing with other children, fending off his sister. This figure would have gone up once his sister went to school, but still.

– school years: about an hour a day, not much, but then they kept you pretty busy; when they were at school Martin and Tom seemed to have much more free time than he ever did.

– at college: four hours a day, if this included pub, watching TV, what the boys now called 'hanging out'.

– first years at work and doing his articles: about an hour a day. Mr Phillips had been so tired he often would make no plans for evenings or weekends, except when he was actively involved in looking for a girlfriend.

Then, once Martin was born and for the next fourteen years while he and Tom were growing up to, say, generously, fifteen minutes a day when at home. (Mrs Phillips even less – indeed she feels the whole time issue much more keenly than Mr Phillips. 'With small children you spend so much time just with them,' she says. 'You're not doing anything, you're just with them. I love them, but it's still a bit much sometimes.') During these years most of the free time Mr Phillips had – time spent without someone making an active demand on him or without doing something he was supposed to be doing – was at work. So the emphasis of free time shifted from home to work. Say he spent one and a half to two hours a day at work not doing anything – pretending to work, looking out of the window, sitting in meetings not listening etc. And once Tom was in full-time school, say four hours a day of nothing time, allowing for the same amount of time at work and considerably more at home. Obviously these are rough figures. So then the calculation would be:

first 5 years	*6 hrs*	*37.5% of waking time*
next 12 years	*1 hr*	*6.25%*
next 3 years	*4 hrs*	*25%*
next 5 years	*1 hr*	*6.25%*
next 14 years	*15 min at home + 1.45 hrs at work = 2 hrs = 12.5%*	
next 11 years	*4 hrs*	*25%*

This works out as a weighted average of 16.375 per cent, or 2.62 hours, or 2 hours and 37 minutes of, broadly speaking, free or nothing time. It is a lot of blank space to account for in one life span. Now that he is redundant he is going to have even more of it; in fact, he can have all day every day, unless and until he finds something else to do. The thought of this is an immense strain. It must be why so many men died after their retirement.

Two of the many foreign coach drivers parked across the road from the Tate are having an argument in a language Mr Phillips does not recognize. They are standing on the roadward side of their huge two-decker vehicles. The shorter and by a fine margin angrier of the two is pointing repeatedly at the other's coach, then at himself, then downwards at the road, while the other man energetically shakes his head and keeps loudly repeating the same word.

Mr Phillips presses on up the road, past the nasty modern building where the Labour Party has its headquarters, into which a dispatch rider has just stridden, past the dwarfing, monolithic government buildings along the Embankment. Further along the road he can see the beginnings of Westminster, all grand and Gothic and trying to look a million years old. If banks try to look all secure and posh and safe and stable and big and respectable and stuffy and built to last for all time, for the simple reason that at heart they are just casinos, what is it that these government buildings were concealing? Probably that they tried to make people feel small, so that the actions of the people in these buildings will seem far beyond their understanding, impersonal and authoritative and independent of anything so trivial as the consent of the governed. It is like Peter Pan only backwards: if we all clapped our hands then the whole edifice of government could be made to go away, to fade like night terrors remembered in sunshine.

As Mr Phillips nears the Houses of Parliament he sees a nice little park across the road. For a moment he wonders if this is where politicians are always being interviewed for the telly, then he realizes it isn't.

'Girl your booty is so round, let me look you up and down,' sings Martin.

He and Mr Phillips are sitting in a very big and noisy restaurant just around the corner from Martin's office in Soho. They are both holding menus which they have not yet opened. The room has bare white walls and one entire window is open to the street, so that the diners' conversation has to compete with the traffic as well as with the coming and going of waiters and the general restaurant hullabaloo. Martin is holding a lit cigarette in his left hand.

'What's that one called?' asks Mr Phillips.

'That's the one that gave me the idea,' explains Martin. 'It's called *Boom Boom Boom* by the Outhere Brothers.'

'Is a booty the same thing as a bottom?' asks Mr Phillips. But his son does not dignify the question with a reply.

'You'd better look at the menu,' says Martin. 'I've got to be back in the office by a quarter past two.'

Mr Phillips has not heard of many of the things on the printed and dated list in front of him. What is lomu and why does it cost £6.95? What is or are couscous, teriyaki, carciofini and bok choy? He could ask Martin, but Martin – although he had seemed pleased enough at his father's unannounced and entirely unexpected lunchtime drop-in – does not now seem in all that good a mood. Mr Phillips settles for grilled scallops with bacon followed by a fish cake.

A waitress wearing black Doc Marten boots, a very short black skirt and a white shirt with two buttons undone comes to their table. Martin says:

'Is it my imagination, Sophie, or are you looking even more beautiful than usual today?'

'What'll it be, Mr Phillips?' says Sophie, blushing only very faintly.

'Martin,' says Martin. 'This is the real Mr Phillips. Sophie – meet my father. Dad – meet Sophie.'

'Hello,' they both say.

'What would you like to eat, Mr Phillips?' Sophie says, this time to Mr Phillips. He gives her his order. She turns swiftly, without speaking, to Martin.

'Well, you know what I want, Sophie,' he says, 'but what I'll eat is the pumpkin ravioli followed by the sea bass. I'll have fizzy water and Dad'll have – gin and tonic?'

'Yes please,' says Mr Phillips. Sophie goes away after volunteering to put ice and lemon in both drinks. Martin sits back happily.

'Tell me about the new record you're doing,' says Mr Phillips. Martin runs his own company. They buy up rights to songs and assemble compilation records based on themes and periods in pop music.

'We haven't decided on the title yet. Something like *Boys on*

Girls, only probably not quite that. The idea is men's songs about women from a politically incorrect point of view. No love songs, just tracks about being randy and fancying girls. "Titties and Beer" – that's a Frank Zappa song – only it's too complicated musically. I mean, musically, it's the sort of thing Mum would approve of.'

'Well, we can't have that,' says Mr Phillips.

'"Get out of my dream and into my car",' says Martin. '"Smack my bitch up".' Then, seeing his father's expression, he explains, 'It's ironic.'

'Ah,' says Mr Phillips.

The restaurant is by now completely full. At Wilkins and Co., Mr Phillips normally ate lunch either in the staff canteen or at his desk, dividing his custom between the two most closely adjacent sandwich bars, both of them run by friendly Italians. This had however become a source of ethical friction, since the nearer (and humanly nicer, by a narrow margin) shop had recently begun to fall away in the quality of its sandwich making – a slightly pongy prawn cocktail sauce one day, a soggy ham bap on a subsequent visit. It was a problem. Should Mr Phillips a. say something, b. switch his custom to the other shop, c. give up eating sandwiches altogether, d. carry on spending money there as usual for old times' sake and out of embarrassment and an inability to walk past the shop to its neighbour and competitor on every single sandwich-eating day? He was too shy for a., not ruthless enough for b., already fat enough for the c. option of eating only canteen food to be a bad idea. But if he did opt for d. out of weakness and sympathy, perhaps he was undermining the efficiency of the free market and damaging the sandwich shop even further, causing them to end up losing more customers because they hadn't been alerted sufficiently early to their budding quality control problems? He would be gumming up the works, making things worse by trying to be nice, like those people who won't take their change from prices which end in 99p, and so unwittingly and well-meaningly contribute to inflation, the cancer of modern economic life, the eroder of savings, destroyer of industry, scourge of the middle class, the force that brought Hitler to power. Or at least that was what he had been taught by the most right-wing of his economics lecturers.

Being sacked had at least solved that dilemma for him.

This restaurant is really something. Mr Phillips has never seen anything like it. Every single customer in the place seems to be talking or shouting as loudly as possible, except for the waiters who are rushing about at dangerous speed, and who seem especially to enjoy the bit where they swivel and bang backwards through the kitchen doors holding their trays stylishly high.

The drinks arrive, Sophie the waitress moving out of flirtation range with polite rapidity.

'Is this what it's normally like here?' Mr Phillips asks.

'Noisier on Fridays, but basically,' says Martin. 'You're going to ask how many of them are paying for themselves, aren't you?'

'I hadn't been, but now that you've brought it up.'

'Next to none.'

'This is my treat, by the way,' says Mr Phillips, who until that very moment has not thought of the question.

'You sure? I could deduct you as a business adviser.'

'I won't hear of it.'

Their first courses arrive. Mr Phillips's portion of bacon and scallops is on the small side but despite, or perhaps for some psychological reason because of that, is delicious. His son, always a very methodical eater, is dividing each of his ravioli in half before chewing and swallowing it.

'How's Tom?'

Martin always asks about Tom and always sounds both patronizing and friendly when he does so. To Mr Phillips, whose relationship with his sister is nothing like what it was when they were both children, it looks as if Martin and Tom will never entirely stop being older and younger brother. Odd to imagine them in their seventies or eighties, with Martin still having this edge over his kid sibling.

'Asleep most of the time. The rest he divides between staying in his room playing horrible music and going out with his friends.'

'Acne any better?'

'No, not much.'

'I was lucky mine was all on my back,' says Martin meditatively, as if this were a very large question to which he belatedly realizes he hadn't given sufficient thought. 'So to what do

I owe the pleasure? What brings you to this part of town?'

Mr Phillips, who has a mouthful of bacon and scallop, gestures with his fork while he swallows his mouthful.

'. . . ing much, just happened to be passing by.'

'At the risk of boasting, you're lucky I can spare the time. Things are manic at the moment. We're on the point of releasing two different dance compilations, negotiating a seventies revival album, and another one of cover versions. It's mental.'

And this had seemed, from the atmosphere of Martin's office, to be true. At the top of a flight of stairs in what would once have been a small town house but was now commercial flats over a sex shop, M Enterprises turned out to be a single room with four people in it, all of them simultaneously on the telephone. When Mr Phillips, who had never been to Martin's office before, walked in, he was slightly out of breath from the climb up the stairs. He stood there feeling embarrassed while the three people who were not Martin looked at him without recognition. Then his son, who had been standing and looking out the window while talking on the phone, turned around and saw him. He raised his eyebrows and smiled but kept talking.

Martin is an even six feet, taller than Mr Phillips himself, and the shuffling of his and Mrs Phillips's genes has given Martin black hair (from Mr Phillips), cheekbones (Mrs Phillips), grey eyes from, apparently, Mrs Phillips's father (dead before they met) and a deceptively athletic figure – 'deceptively' because Martin, unlike his younger brother, disliked all exercise. Having worn deliberately rebellious clothes all through his school days, as ripped and unkempt as possible, he is now wearing a single breasted grey suit, dark blue shirt and rather subtle maroon tie, all of which make him look older. If he were not Mr Phillips's son, Mr Phillips realizes, there would not have been the slightest chance that he and Martin could ever have met. And perhaps an equally small chance that they would have had anything to say to each other.

When he finally got off the telephone Martin said:

'Dad! To what do I owe the pleasure? Dad – this is everyone. Everyone – this is Dad.'

The other people in the office, all of whom were still holding phones, raised a hand and nodded or made some other gesture of recognition without stopping what they were doing. Two of them were unusually pretty girls. The effect was not so much of deliberate rudeness but of an attempt at politely suppressing their curiosity. It was one of those moments when Mr Phillips feels like an alien, like a spy, or like someone who has adopted a cover story so successfully that he is beginning to forget who he is or used to be. His uniform of class and profession seemed baggy, as if he could slip out of it at any moment with a single convulsive wriggle; while at the same time he could feel his stomach pressing against his belt buckle, asking that it be let out another notch. He has a memory of his father putting on blue overalls and contentedly going off to work with his bag of tools and pipe – he had loved his electrician's costume, had taken great comfort from it. What would we do without uniforms?

Mr Phillips sometimes feels that other men have something he doesn't have and – he has to conclude, as he gets stuck into his sixth decade – will never have. This is the carapace which grows or solidifies around them as they get older, and which involves an increasing lack of uncertainty about, or interest in, anything they don't already know ('know' being defined as something like 'feel that they have fully comprehended, to their own satisfaction'). Mr Mill, for instance, Mr Phillips's former head of department, has a hardness to him, a rigidity, that is nothing to do with determination or resolve or strength of character or anything other than a philosophical impermeability, a thick skin. Nothing new is ever likely to reach him. Told about a development in corporate procedures that would affect hundreds of his colleagues but not him – a new way of calculating overtime rates, say, which would cost most of them £500 a year, but about which they were prevented from striking by fresh government legislation, crashed though Parliament in a specific attempt to alter practices at Wilkins and Co. – he would, once he had established that the change had no direct effect on him, stop paying any attention. He would react with the polite but obdurate impassivity of a Catholic cardinal temporarily trapped into sitting next to a UFO enthusiast at a wedding reception. To Mr Phillips this is not admirable, but it is enviable.

Mr Phillips's father had that carapace. Something inside him had sunk and retreated. There was a wariness. His solitariness and holding back always made him alien, a stranger;

and perhaps electricians as a profession have something reserved about them, the caution of men used to dealing with a far larger power which was always capable of administering nasty surprises. Any plan or intention of the young Mr Phillips – a plan to travel to watch Crystal Palace play away from home, go to a friend's party or to the cinema, his initial announcement of wanting to stay on at school and do A levels, the subsequent announcement that he wanted to be a chartered accountant, his first visit to the bank to borrow money to buy a car, even his heading into the kitchen to offer token help to his mother – was greeted with the words, 'Why do you want to do that?' – not so much a question as a disrecommendation or even a warning. The caution came across as a kind of hardness. Martin, at twenty-five, was already starting to grow his own more modern brand of the same thing.

'Do you have any plans for lunch?' Mr Phillips asked his son and then, suddenly quailing at the thought of being alone with him, said, 'And of course if any of your colleagues . . .'

'They're all too busy,' said Martin. 'And so would I be if that prat from A and J records hadn't stood me up. Thanks. I'd love to. There's a place I go to a lot, and might be able to score us a table even though we haven't booked. I've just got a couple of calls to make. Have a sit down and I'll be with you in two ticks.' Although Martin would not have wanted his father to notice that he was trying to impress him, he noticed it nonetheless. One of the surprising things about Martin was that he was in many respects still rather young.

Mr Phillips picked up the book that was lying on his son's desk. It was called *Hitler Wins! Management Skills of Germany's Greatest Leader (And Don't Let Anybody Tell You Different)*. The page was turned down at the start of a chapter called 'Don't Think Different, Think Beyond.'

'What's this?' he asked.

'It's the management book everybody's reading at the moment,' said Martin. 'There's always one – you know, lateral thinking, *Seven Habits of Highly Effective People*, *Winning Through Intimidation*, all that crap. They're mainly bollocks but it gives you something to talk about. Go ahead and have a look, I'll just be a minute.'

Mr Phillips opened the book in the middle.

Hitler envisaged a united Europe. He envisaged a world in which the motorist would be able to travel from Calais to Zagreb on motorways. He foresaw German hegemony, as the dominant power of the continent. He was a vegetarian at a time and in a milieu when that was a strange thing to be. (He pointed out that 'Japanese wrestlers, who live off nothing but vegetables, are among the strongest men in the world.' This also goes to prove that the Führer was willing to consider lessons and examples from other, far-away cultures – an important example for any leader in today's globally competitive environment.)

All these are examples of what it takes to be a visionary thinker, one who sees beyond conventional patterns of thought and behaviour. They show you that you are often right by being wrong;

by saying the opposite of what others say, confident in the validity of your own insights. They also show us that we must look to the broadest perspectives to see our ideas bear fruit. Like the Führer we must be confident that posterity will vindicate us. (See Chapter 10, for 'How to Have Your Posterity Today'.) As we look at today's Europe, united and dominated by a recrudescent Germany, in which we can travel on motorways from Calais to Seville, from Boulogne to Athens, which of us can look into our hearts and say that the Führer was in any meaningful sense wrong?

THIS IS THE WAY IN WHICH A SUCCESSFUL BUSINESS MANAGER MUST LEARN TO THINK.

Martin swung his jacket off the back of the chair and was already heading towards his father and the exit.

Somewhere in Mr Phillips's mind, when he decided to pop in on Martin, had been the notion that he might be able to confide in his elder son about what had happened. But as soon as he saw Martin he felt that it wouldn't be possible, not so much because of the admission of weakness on his own part that would be involved, but because Martin in some hard to define but real way would not be strong enough to bear the news. (It's a proverb: when the father helps the son, both smile; when the son helps the father, both cry.) He might laugh or weep or do some other inappropriate thing. Did some men have sons with whom that kind of exchange might be imaginable? Mr Phillips remembers the first time his mother had given him a jam jar to twist open and said, 'Don't tell Dad.'

'You're going to be rich,' says Mr Phillips, meaning it not as a compliment but as a fact.

'Depends what you mean by rich.'

'Richer than Mum and me, anyway.'

'Well, yeah. Obviously.'

It takes Mr Phillips a second to realize that this is a joke. Their main courses have by now arrived. Mr Phillips finishes his G and T.

'How's Mum?'

'Very well. Same as ever.'

'Doesn't sound as if much has been happening.'

'Well, you know how it is.'

'It's a funny feeling, in some ways,' says Martin. 'The idea of being rich. Especially since it'll only happen if someone comes in and buys up the company. I mean, that's basically the only way you can suddenly get a ton of money dumped on you overnight. So you sell the company and then what? The main thing you've been doing for years is taken away. So what you do is start another company and start all over again. It's like sex.'

'Is it?' asked Mr Phillips.

'You know, love them and leave them. But that's only an idea, a saying, it's not like official.'

'What sort of money?'

'A bloke who was doing a fairly similar thing with retro compilations was bought up for half a million. Anything can happen. In three years' time, I'll either be going home from work to Notting Hill in a brand new Beamer, or taking the Northern Line back to Morden and trying to dodge the fare. It could go either way.'

Mr Phillips, who had taken the train in to Waterloo every working day for the last twenty-six years until this morning, digests that in silence.

'This is very nice,' he says, offering some fish cake on the end of his fork. The fish cake is not as good as Mrs Mitchinson's, but it isn't bad. Martin, who is chewing, shakes his head and nods down at his plate. Mr Phillips declines the offer to try his son's expensive-looking piece of grilled fish.

'Those are pretty girls you have working for you,' he says.

'You fugga da staff, you fugga da business. You must know that – it's an old Italian saying. But yeah, they're all right. Debbie, the blonde one, is the toughest. She can shave points like no one you've ever seen. Now *she's* going to be rich one day, for sure.'

When the waitress comes back, Martin says, 'I'm at a loss for words again, Sophie. Let me take you away from all this.'

'Would you like any dessert or coffee at all?' says Sophie.

They settle on two coffees and the bill. Mr Phillips feels the weight of things bearing down on him more heavily than he has at any point since his conversation with Mr Wilkins. The idea of having nothing to do, an empty diary, an empty life, stretching out in front of him until he dies. Luckily at that moment the bill arrives. Sums come to the rescue. Ravioli at £6.95, bacon and scallops at £6.75, fish cake at £8, sea bass at £12, large mineral water £2.50, gin and tonic £3.50, two filter coffees £4, service at 12.5 per cent is £5.46, equals £49.16. Six plus seven is thirteen, eight plus twelve is twenty, which makes thirty-three, two fifty plus three fifty is six, plus four is ten, plus thirty-three is forty-three, plus the fiver for service is forty-eight, which is close enough once you've added in the pennies. Mr Phillips fishes out his cheque book and begins to write. His son picks up the bill and looks at it.

'Good value here,' he says. 'For this part of town. Do you mind if I love you and leave you? Only I know I've got a call coming in at quarter past on the dot.'

'By all means,' says Mr Phillips. They shake hands, Martin gets up and is gone with a final 'Love to Mum' over his shoulder.

So that was Martin. Mr Phillips waits for Sophie to come back and take the bill. Instead it is another waitress who comes and picks up the bill and cheque and cheque card, and a third who brings it back, pressing his plastic card back on to the table with a brisk click and equivalently brisk pro forma smile. Both these girls are good looking, the first a leggy, slightly ungainly dyed blonde, black hair visible at the roots of her parting, distracted, sexy; the other shorter, darker, slightly cross-looking, heavier around the middle and lower half, verging on the outright bottomy, but sexy too. Her bad temper made you wonder what her good temper would be like; what it would be like to be fucking her, see her expression and compare it with her normal cross face. That was probably what men who liked cross girls liked about them.

Taken with the lovely Sophie and with Martin's colleagues

144

that was a lot of pretty girls for one lunchtime. If you were a Martian walking around earth in disguise you would form an inaccurate impression of how many pretty girls there were if you went by how many of them you encountered in public places as waitresses, receptionists, front-of-house people, the people you dealt with when you went to offices or shops or pubs or restaurants. Anywhere, basically, where there was an opportunity to put a pretty girl in between you and a transaction. So pretty girls were a kind of consumable substance, used up like fuel, or used like WD40 to ease the mechanisms. And there's always a fresh supply, that's the beauty of it.

Mr Phillips decides to go for a pee, not so much because he needs one, more as a precaution. The fact of his not needing one, itself unusual, is a sign of how hot the day is, how much he must be sweating. He weaves through tables towards the back of the restaurant where the loos are. The place is thinning out now, and about half the tables are empty, people reluctantly dragging themselves back to work; of the lunchers who stay behind, a fair few of them look as if they are set for the long haul, with second or third bottles of wine being broached, brandies appearing, chairs being pushed back. Two of the tables have what look like courting couples sitting at them, holding hands and looking at each other. None of them seems at all married. Or not to each other, anyway. In the case of one couple, the man is at least twice his girlfriend's age. Lucky devil! Well done! If he is married to someone else, he must be confident that this is the kind of place he can come to without any news of what's going on getting back to anyone who knows him. Given that there must be a couple of hundred people passing through the restaurant at any one mealtime, that would seem to Mr Phillips to be a statistically significant risk.

The toilets are down a little white-walled corridor. Mr Phillips has a faint dread about whether or not he will be able to tell the Gents and the Ladies apart, but in the event it is straightforward: the Gents is demarcated by a cartoon dandy holding a monocle to his eye with his left hand and brandishing a cocked duelling pistol in his right. He wears a top hat and tails and a confident, supercilious expression. So that's easy enough, even though anyone who looks less like Mr Phillips feels would be hard to imagine. The Ladies has a woman in a huge hooped ball gown that she is ever so slightly hitching up to reveal a glimpse of well-turned ankle.

Mr Phillips pushes the door, goes in, unzips his trousers, releases his penis from his Y-fronts, and begins to pee. It is a surprisingly unmodern urinal given the rest of the restaurant décor, a long marble stand-alongside. After half a century of visiting urinals, Mr Phillips is still uncertain whether the little built-up ledge is supposed to be used for standing on and peeing downwards, or for standing behind and peeing over, which is more protective of the pee-er's feet but also messier since drops inevitably splosh on the ledge. In Mr Phillips's experience other men don't know what to do either, or at least there is no consistent pattern, or (at the very least) two schools of thought.

The bright blue medicinal balls in the bottom of the urinal give off a sharp chemical smell as they come into contact with Mr Phillips' unusually dark, almost ochre, urine. When he does his trousers up Mr Phillips notices their increased after-lunch tightness. His stomach presses against the waistband with a friendly pressure, like a man laying a respectful rather than a lascivious hand on his wife's bottom.

The street outside the restaurant is very busy. It can't get any hotter. This is the kind of weather Mr Phillips's father had loved – 'It's good to sweat,' he would say cheerfully, striding away up a hill on an August expedition to the country with his shirt soaked through in the small of his back.

Not far from where Mr Phillips is standing there is, he knows, the White Hart, the pub where, going out for a drink with some colleagues from Grimshaw's, he met the future Mrs Phillips for the first time. She was part of a group of girls at the bar to whom he and his friends got talking when one of them spilt a Pernod and blackcurrant on somebody's trousers. Not that it was love at first sight: tall and brown haired with a high, wide forehead, pretty but not overwhelmingly so, brainy-looking, she wasn't precisely Mr Phillips's type, since in those days he liked, or thought he liked, obviously tarty-looking girls, ideally blonde or, failing that, black-haired, shorter than him, with the emphasis more on the bum than the tits though not dogmatically so. He had a tendency to fall for girls to whom he could explain things. But for some reason, girls to whom he could explain things did a very good job of not falling for him.

Mrs Phillips, on the other hand, not only seemed to be better informed than him on most artistic and political subjects, she also knew London better, or knew more parts of it, and she also knew what she wanted to do – which was play, teach, and listen to music. It was not something she went on about or showed off about but it was there, and Mr Phillips to his great surprise found this a turn-on. The first time he saw her playing the clarinet, her subsidiary instrument after the piano, at a concert in a church in Islington, he got an enormous erection – it was in that moment that she became, for him, fully charged sexually. At the same time, she seemed actually to like him, which, he realized, quite a few of his other girlfriends hadn't. He hadn't liked them much either. Meeting the future Mrs Phillips made him realize that this was not necessarily how things were supposed to be.

'You seemed so lost,' she said, years later, explaining why she had taken to him. The first time they made love, at her shared flat on a Saturday night when her Scottish flatmate had gone home for the weekend to celebrate her parents' wedding anniversary, she had insisted on keeping her socks on, which Mr Phillips had found more intimate and revealing than if she had been starkers.

'But what if I had wanted to keep mine on?' he asked afterwards.

'I would have kicked you out.'

'There's a double standard at work,' said Mr Phillips.

The shop Mr Phillips is standing in front of sells leather

clothes, and advertises itself as a 'clone zone'. It takes him a second or two to realize that it is aiming at a clientele of homosexual men. Once he does realize, he becomes self-conscious and begins to move away, though not without wishing he didn't feel self-conscious, so he could settle down for a proper look. It would not do to give people the wrong impression: but what were 'poppers'? And why would anyone want to have his nipples pierced?

The shop next door has a grotto-like entrance, painted a luscious dark vaginal red. A bored-looking girl – pretty girl again – with short dark bobbed hair sits behind a sort of counter, painting her nails pink and looking up occasionally to address encouraging remarks to potential customers. Live Sex Shows XXXX says a sign above her head. Behind her and to one side is a plastic curtain.

'Your heart's desire is inside,' says the girl to Mr Phillips, so matter-of-factly that it gives him a strange jolting thrill; by being so uninterested in what she is saying she makes him feel as if it might be true. If a woman's business was sex there could be something sexy about her not being all that interested or bothered about it. Part of Mr Phillips, quite a large part, wants to push past that plastic curtain and go into the grotto. But he feels too shy, and as if he would somehow be exposing himself. So he sidles past trying to look casual.

It is hard to walk down this street without being made to think about sex. The number of gay businesses is striking, once Mr Phillips realizes that that is what they are – the bar called Spartacus, for instance, and the coffee shop, spilling out into the fumes and dirt of the pavement, none-too-subtly called Gay Paree. There are also plenty of straightforward sex shops or 'Adult Shops', not as explicit in their window displays as they would have been a few years ago, but now in a way worse because they have words like 'xxx' and 'Sex Toys' and 'Videos' and 'Adults Only' and 'Explicit Material Inside' and 'DO NOT ENTER Unless You Are Not Shocked By Sexually Explicit Material' and all the other enticements. Mr Fortesque was right. Sex is a good steady business to be in, Mr Phillips can see that.

When his father had died in 1981, of a stroke, Mr Phillips had helped his mother clear out his parents' small house – not the one Mr Phillips had grown up in in Wandsworth but a newer, bigger semi in Sutton. It was a bad time. Mr Phillips disliked sorting through old things anyway, because his overwhelmingly strong instinct never to throw anything away made it difficult for him to take rational decisions; he ended up lingering over and fingering old calendars, old rail tickets, car magazines, bank statements. In the course of the Phillips's periodic blitzes on Martin's and Tom's rooms, he would be more reluctant to chuck out old clothes and old posters than they were themselves. Mr Phillips liked to think this was linked to the trained accountant's fear of mislaying an important piece of paper. At the same time, he felt a powerful impulse to cling on to everything, to keep the past alive by maintaining a physical grip on objects whose meaning belonged there.

'You're a squirrel,' was what his mother had said. It struck him as a startling metaphor.

'Am I?'

'It's just an expression.'

'They're vermin, aren't they? Squirrels.'

'It's just an expression.'

His father too had been a squirrel; his mother on the other hand was a . . . whatever the opposite of a squirrel was. It was hard to think of an animal that took active pleasure in throwing things out. Something small and clever and quick, which didn't keep things stashed in its burrow.

The result was that the house, when they went through it in the aftermath of his father's death, had been full of his things but had almost nothing of his mother's. It was as if she had died a while before. There didn't seem to be any distinctions or discrimination in his father's hoarding. One trunk had carried both his own father's birth certificate, which by any standards was an important piece of paper, along with ten years of Mr Phillips's and his sister's school reports, carried in a Manila envelope that was itself stained with age.

The bottom drawers of his father's desk, one on each side, had been locked. The key was in the supposedly secret drawer at the back of the middle part of the desk, just above where your knees went – though it was hard to imagine a burglar so idle or so useless that he wouldn't find the hiding place within seconds. The left-hand drawer had contained up to date financial records and two National Savings certificates to the tune of £5000 each – which, with the house, proved to be the out-standing bulk of his father's estate, enabling Mrs Phillips to move to Australia to live with Mavis and Terry and the girls. The marriage certificate, from Wandsworth registry office, and Mr Phillips's grandmother's death certificate were also there, in a folder marked 'Certificates'. The drawer on the other side had been full of pornographic magazines and pictures cut out of pornographic magazines, some of which had been put in a clear plastic folder because . . . because what? They were his father's favourites and he didn't want them to be damaged by his own fingering?

Mr Phillips could not stop himself from paying close atten-tion to this glimpse into his father's consciousness. At the same time, he had to admit that he wouldn't want his sons to have the same opportunity in relation to him –

'Dad wasn't much of a tit man, was he?'

'No, it was bums or nothing for the old man.'

His father did however seem to have been a tit man. How odd that these things weren't inherited or genetically pro-grammed. The photos encased in plastic were not, Mr Phillips was confident, the ones that he himself would have chosen. You would have thought that if any preference or affinity was going to be inherited it would be that.

His father had died too soon: these days there were whole magazines dedicated to the subject of big breasts. Though that might have been too much of a good thing; perhaps flicking through the pages looking for a just-right girl was part of the thrill of the chase. But Michael Phillips had been forced to look at photos of girls bending over to show off their bottoms, or lying on their backs looking as if they wanted to have sex right there and then – which was fine in Mr Phillips's book, but did tend to make their breasts look smaller. In the drawer there must have been thirty magazines, featuring naked girls in not too explicit poses – no 'beaver shots' of gaping vulvas. Say ten girls a magazine, so a total of three hundred girls in his father's version of Bluebeard's room. In addition, there were another forty or so girls encased in the plastic. So that was 340 in all, hidden in his father's desk drawer. The girls would have gone on with their lives, some of them presumably making reasonable livings in modelling, others quitting young, or having one big break, this session with *Knave* or *Penthouse* or *Mayfair* the apogee of their careers, since what did they do next? Were they endlessly recycled among the top magazines, or was it one brief moment literally under the lights and then finito? Anyway, their lives would have gone on, the photo session a vague or vivid or unhappy or deliberately suppressed memory, while they lived on fixedly in his father's desk drawer, caught for all time in a momentary pose adopted who knew where, who knew when, in front of who knew what sort of sleazy, grimacing patter-keeping-up photographer. 'Make love to the camera! Show me your heat!'

The strength of the appetites represented by this pile of images had its impressive side. But finding the photos made Mr Phillips feel lonely. His grief he had to some extent been able to share with his wife (who had liked his father, and thought he was 'a good man') and mother and sister, who had flown over for the funeral but only stayed for thirty-six hours, since she had had to return for some pressing family reason Mr Phillips could not now remember. But he didn't feel he could share his discovery with any of them; it was against the ethics of male fellowship, as well as against family feeling, as well as the opposite of what his father would have wanted. So he put the magazines and clippings and plastic folders along with other throwoutable items into a big plastic bag and headed for the council dump. There was a not-small touch of death in this, since papers which his father by definition hadn't thrown out had now become, at the moment of his death, junk, rubbish, clutter, their interpretable status changing through no fault of their own. He chose the dump, rather than just leaving them out for collection by the bin men, in case one of the bags might split open and disgorge its mixture of old bills, old bank statements, old newspapers and pictures of naked women to the astonished and secretly thrilled street. I always thought there was something odd about him.

The plan was to take the clothes to Oxfam; other saleable items, like the radio his father had kept in the bathroom, a dressing-table mirror with a hideous pink frame, and other things that neither his wife nor Mrs Phillips wanted, to the Barnardo's charity shop; papers and pornography to the dump. Mr Phillips drove to the dump first, because he was troubled by the possibility that he might hand the wrong bags over by mistake. A man from the council in blue overalls was directing traffic at the site, over which hung a faint smell of burning and the stronger, sweet reek of dumped rubbish. As he began hefting the bags out of the car Mr Phillips realized that he didn't trust them to stay intact until they were thrown into the masher or incinerated or whatever happened to them. Again, the worry was that the bags might be torn open and the contents strewn around by the wind or whatever else, and his father's secrets would be revealed, and at the same time, because of the bank statements and utility bills, his identity might be traceable, so that everyone would know who he was and what he had liked. So, having got to the dump, Mr Phillips returned the bags back to the back of the car and drove home, by now in Saturday post-football traffic. He made a melodramatic bonfire in his own back garden, banning Mrs Phillips and the children from going outside. He stacked up the magazines, took the pictures out of their plastic holders and crumpled them on top, poured barbecue lighter fluid over the lot and threw on a match. The mountains of girls in their stiff paper, the curious waxy paper of porn mags, burned well. Then he put the other, innocuous papers into the rubbish bin at the front of the house, the last time his father's stuff would be taken away by the bin men, and went back inside. The clothes and odd and ends stayed in the car, since it was by now too late to take them to their respective charities.

'You smell of smoke,' Mrs Phillips said when he came in. She had repeatedly offered to help.

'Just a few odds and ends,' said Mr Phillips, thinking of his momentary panic when a fragment of burning girl – the upper half of a blonde with big tits, his father's type – had begun to rise on the flames, up to head height, so that for a second it looked as if she might be carried away on the breeze into a neighbour's garden, until the updraught of hot air failed her and she sank, charred and unrecognizable now, just beyond the outer edges of the pyre.

Mr Phillips is now standing across the road from a shop that has the word Videos written in dark crimson on a pink shutter; it also has the plastic curtains which seem big in this market sector. Beside the shop entrance is another doorway with a flight of stairs visible inside it. The word Films is written above the lintel. People are milling about, apparently not paying much attention to one another, in that deceptive London way which can mean that they aren't paying attention, or that they are sizing each other up. Sex and violence are always possible. Two men in shorts and vests, both with cropped blond hair, walk past. Mr Phillips has to concede that they are better dressed for the weather than he himself is. Another man, squat and cheerful, is standing beside the sex shop calling out 'Big Issue' and holding a copy of the magazine in front of his chest as if he were advertising not it but himself.

Mr Phillips takes his courage in his hands and crosses the street, pushes through the curtain and goes into the sex shop. It is a square box of a room with magazines on two walls, a display cabinet on the third and a counter on the fourth. There are two other customers, both men, and a bored, grumpy fat man at the till. Both of the men are leafing through magazines with a flushed listlessness.

Mr Phillips moves over to one of the stands of magazines while casting sideways looks at the third wall, which seems mainly to consist of objects made to look like penises – dildoes and vibrators. There is also a box with the words 'edible underwear' written on it, another box labelled 'tit clamps' and a third box that says simply 'one size fits all'. One or two of the dildoes are remarkably big – in context, perhaps the biggest things Mr Phillips has ever seen. It is a long time since he has seen penises in any significant numbers, since the showers at St Aloysius's in fact, but his memories on the point are pretty clear, and they are that although penises look very much unlike each other, more so than even their owners (if that was the word), they don't vary all that much in size – especially when compared to breasts, which vary wildly, and in wholly unpredictable ways. Small girls have big tits, big girls have invisible tits, and every permutation in between, most of them employing the three basic shapes of the dome, the turret, and the hillock. Penises are not like that. In the language of statistics, they are tightly grouped about the mean. So these dildoes in Mr Phillips's opinion are at the least statistically unrepresentative or at the worst wild flights of fantasy.

A large sign over the magazine rack says 'Try Before You Buy is *Not* Our Policy.' Mr Phillips feels too shy to actually pick up any of the magazines so he merely stands and looks at the covers. *Dutch Hardcore xxx* is the name of the magazine that the man next to him is reading. He is wearing a black donkey jacket and seems half asleep. There are many titles that would have suited Mr Phillips's father. *Big Tits, Jugs, Hooters!* and *Party Tits* are some of the examples. Mr Phillips thinks he can confirm his impressions about unrepresentative penis size by looking at one of the gay or hardcore magazines, but he doesn't feel quite strong enough. Cautiously, with a growing sense that he is doing something he is not supposed to do, he reaches out for a copy of *Anal Action* magazine, telling himself that he is looking to see if it is what he thinks it is. He opens the magazine at random and finds himself faced with a full-page photograph of a penis inserted halfway inside a woman's rectum. The woman's unoccupied vulva is visible too, but no other part of either protagonist. There is something shocking but also almost abstract about the picture. So much has been left out. The picture does not describe sex or evoke it; it doesn't make Mr Phillips imagine what that would be like to do, merely leaves him numb in the face of its having been done. The colours – the healthy pink of the woman's bottom, the darker purply pink of the man's penis and the bruised reddish-brown aureole of the penetrated anus – are almost the main feature. The photographer's task, his face and camera pressed close to the flesh of the performers, must have been a strange one. Mr Phillips feels dazed, aroused, oddly flat.

He closes the magazine and walks out of the shop, sensing glances on his back as he goes. He pushes through the plastic curtain and takes a sharp right U-turn through the door marked Films. A steep, not especially well lit or well maintained flight of stairs leads him upwards into a bigger, hall-like area in which a girl sits behind a kiosk chatting to a heavy-set man in a leather jacket. There are posters for films on the wall. A three-quarters naked woman in a white dress with a very strange hairstyle – it looks as if she had bread rolls in her ears – carrying a science fiction pistol in her left hand and pointing it very close up in front of her mouth, is advertising a film called *Star Whores*. A woman apparently wearing no clothes is lying head to toe on top of a man, also naked, in front of a flying saucer piloted by a cartoon space alien, with bug eyes and little antennae, who is looking down at them. That one is called *Close Encounters of the Sixty-Ninth Kind*. A poster frame labelled Showing Today is empty. Mr Phillips, feeling hotter than at any other point in the day, goes across to the kiosk and says to the girl:

'I'd like a ticket for one please.'

The girl, who is chewing gum, says, 'Members only.'

'Oh,' says Mr Phillips, who has a feeling that things are somehow not going to prove quite as simple as he had hoped. He begins to turn away and the girl says, using the kind of voice normally reserved for not very bright children, 'You can join.'

'Oh,' says Mr Phillips again. 'How much?'

'Twenty-four hour membership is £8.50.'

Mr Phillips begins to reach for his wallet.

'Plus the film is £5,' says the girl, who at one level and despite her apparent detachment clearly enjoys her work. Mr Phillips with sweaty hands passes over a £20 note. She takes a small cash box out of a drawer in her kiosk and puts the £20 under a little tray inside it before counting out his £6.50 change. Is VAT included? Not the kind of question you could ask. She hands over a scrappy ticket torn off a blue roll, like a bus ticket bought from a conductor. She also gives Mr Phillips a piece of cardboard with the words Temporary Member stamped on it. The man in the leather jacket – giving Mr Phillips a hard, I'll-recognize-you-next-time look, which Mr Phillips feels breaches the porn cinema's implied and desired ethic of anonymity – tears the ticket in half and lets Mr Phillips through into the small auditorium that is down three or four steps. Thinking about it, Mr Phillips realizes he is either above the sex shop he was in moments before, or perhaps over the shop next door; it is like being in a small grubby labyrinth.

Mr Phillips is in luck. A film is just beginning. It is called *Jim MacTool and the Salmon of Wisdom*. The lights have gone down and he has to manoeuvre his way to a seat under the glow of the flickering screen. About a dozen men are sitting in the room, each of them carefully self-quarantined in his own group of seats.

The film is set in a not very convincing version of Ireland, a rugged landscape with very tall trees. Jim, the hero, is played by a large, deeply tanned blond actor with muscles so big they look as if they have been pumped full of air. He wears a kilt, carries an animal fur on his shoulders and wields a club. Mr Phillips feels that the filmmakers can be relied on to get all of these details wrong. Jim is quite game about trying an Irish accent though about half-way through the film he gives up, or was told to stop, and begins speaking American.

At the start of the film Jim the hero is wandering around on an unnamed quest when he meets a blind old man sitting beside a river with a fishing rod. The man moves to cast his line, loses his footing and falls in, and Jim rescues him. Then they sit around a fire talking. The wise old man tells Jim of his lifelong search for a famous fish called the Salmon of Wisdom. 'He who shall have first taste of the flesh of this fish shall know the wisdom of all things,' says the man. So Jim says he will help the man and the man makes him promise that he will let the man have the first bite of the fish once they have caught and cooked it, since only the first bite allows the eater knowledge of all things. Jim agrees.

The next day the two of them go fishing together and surprise surprise catch a fish which the old man immediately realizes is the Salmon of Wisdom. The two of them fight the fish and land it. The old man, beside himself with excitement, tells Jim to make a fire and settles down to cook the salmon. When the salmon is cooked, Jim goes to take it off the fire but he is over-eager in picking it up and the pain of the heat made him drop the fish into his lap, where it lands in his naked crotch and burns him. He cries out in pain, picks the fish up out of his lap and dumps it into the plate in front of the old man. The old man asks what has happened, and when Jim tells him bursts into tears and says that now Jim's flesh has been burnt by the salmon he has the secret of wisdom every time he sucks the affected piece of flesh. And Jim explains that he has been burnt in a place he cannot suck and that he is the most wretched of men. 'No, the second most wretched,' says the old man, who then drops dead. Jim buries him.

The next day Jim continues his travels and meets a woman who is weeping at a crossroads. She too is blonde, wearing a big black shawl that is partly wrapped around her head in a sort of cowl. She speaks with a thick American accent. She is sad because she is a widow and because her landlord is going to evict her and she can't think of anything to do. So Jim is sad with her but then says that maybe he has an idea, and he explains about the Salmon of Wisdom and what has happened and says that although he cannot consult the salmon himself, anyone sucking the affected area will have knowledge of all things. So with great alacrity the beautiful young widow says that she thinks it is worth a try, and sinks to her knees in front of Jim and lifts up his kilt to reveal a penis that seems, like the rest of Jim, to have been lifting weights and exercising. (Was this possible? Surely not. Jim's penis is large but not comically or terrifyingly so – it is merely very big and rather tanned.) And then the widow slips off her shawl and Jim takes off his kilt, though not his animal fur or his boots, and they have sex in several different ways. The whole Salmon of Wisdom thing is discreetly dropped.

The disconcerting thing about this is that the sex goes on for as long as the rest of the film hitherto, about ten minutes, and that whereas the acting has been bad but touching in its amateurishness (his accent, her attempts at injecting her speech about the evil landlord with real feeling), the sex is mechanical and professional, and is clearly what the people involved are best at and do for a living, while being at the same time so stylized that it, like the *Anal Action* photo Mr Phillips has just seen, is almost abstract. Jim holds his body well clear of the Beautiful Young Widow so that the viewers can see his penis penetrating her vagina, as if his cock were a fleshy piston. The close-up footage of the penis going into and out of the vagina, at a steady rate of, according to Mr Phillips's measurements, about three thrusts per second, is particularly disorientating. The appearance of the act looks completely different from how it feels (assuming that Mr Phillips remembers it correctly). A ten-foot penis going into and out of a two-foot-diameter vagina doesn't in Mr Phillips's opinion correspond to any known human sensation. The penis is so sinisterly knobbled and distorted, the vagina and engorged clitoris so repellently slick, that the whole thing looks somehow inhuman; this act, Mr Phillips realizes, is all about hydraulics.

When younger Mr Phillips would probably have envied this man his work, the endless succession of sex. To spend so much of your life inside vaginas would have seemed hard to beat at nineteen, twenty-four, thirty, even forty. That was when sex seemed like the only thing in the world – which was still, in Mr Phillips's opinion, a perfectly reasonable view, though not one he continued to share. Now he is better able to imagine pitfalls and difficulties: this being one of the things at which you got better as you got older. Take Aids, for one thing. He worries about it enough on behalf of Martin. The porn stars don't look or act as if they have given it a thought but then they wouldn't, would they? And then having to get erections on demand: is there a knack to it or is it a skill you are born with? And if you got an erection on demand did it feel like a normal erection – did you want to do the same things with it – or was it more somehow impersonal, an indifferent appendage for tool-using purposes, like mankind's famous opposable thumb? And then what would you do about normal sex, would that be distinguishable from work?

Is this single sex act genuine, with the camera – which swoops in close, hovers above and circles around the coupling couple – being moved in between shots while they stop and start, or is it lots of separate fucks edited together? Mr Phillips knows that he will never know. At the moment of climax, Jim withdraws his penis from the woman, moves up until he is squatting more or less over her breasts, and masturbates until he squirts semen over her huge wobbly breasts while she looks ecstatic, as if this is what she had in mind all along, her very favourite thing.

The sex in the film has almost no relationship with sex as actually practised but it has important unbreakable rules of its own. Jim does it with a pair of sisters who can't find a way to raise dowry money, an Indian princess who has been ship-wrecked and has to build a boat to sail home, a mother and daughter team in a wattle hut, four nuns who interrupt their own lesbian orgy to – in what quickly becomes Jim's invariably successful chat-up line – 'consult the salmon'. All of these encounters end with Jim ejaculating on or over the women. This is evidently a fixed convention of the genre, as securely defiant of actuality as the hero's unemptyable gun in a Western. It has to be one major difference between sex for recreation and for work, since being able to ejaculate inside someone would in itself count as a major treat. Also, it seems to Mr Phillips, there are fairly obvious variations on the theme of the Salmon of Wisdom that are remaining unexploited, for reasons of taste or lack of imagination: the theme of Jim consulting the salmon for himself, for example, something which double-jointed people, yoga experts etc. were supposed to be able to do. Or Jim's salmon being consulted by other men, say an undergraduate needing help with his exams. Or even Jim allowing the old man to consult the salmon as an ambiguous consolation prize? Again, there is a sense that the rules of the genre are arbitrarily and too strictly defined. The only one of the actresses who really gets to Mr Phillips is the younger of the two sisters, a dark haired girl whose exciting air of normality is enhanced by the fact that she has smallish breasts and a seemingly less professional attitude to the sex – it looks like her second or third time in front of the cameras, as opposed to her second or third thousandth. Her response to the task of performing cunnilingus on her 'sister' (while being penetrated from behind by Jim, naturally) also has something real to it, a reluctance combined with curiosity or the other way around;

unless this is what Mr Phillips so much wants to believe that he is making it up. Might it be the first time she has ever kissed another woman's vagina? She'd said in audition that she was willing to, acted like the request had been no big deal, and was now finding that it was more of an event, physically and psychologically, than she had expected, alien-familiar, fishy-salty-sweet; she looks like someone conscious of being, in a deep inner part of herself, a dirty girl. Mr Phillips likes that. Also, she talks less and makes less noise during sex than the other girls, which also makes her seem more amateurish, which in Mr Phillips's view, in this context, is a virtue.

Mr Phillips can feel that he has an erection and at the same time is very embarrassed, while also realizing that it is odd to feel embarrassed while sitting unobservably in the near-dark. He feels that if he were burst in on – by a police raid, for instance – he might literally die of embarrassment. For that reason and because the novelty is beginning to wear off, Mr Phillips gets up, at the beginning of a scene where Jim has fallen in with three other wandering heroes who are all about to come to the rescue of a tribe of Amazon-type women who are having trouble with a sorcerer. Mass consultation of the salmon is clearly about to occur. Mr Phillips sidles, one of the few times in his life he has ever consciously sidled, through the exit, into the dark tattiness of the ticket hall, where the girl is still chewing gum, the bouncer-cum-ticket collector still standing blankly silent. Then he goes down into the full daylit seediness of the street below.

168

It is half past three. In the office this was Mr Phillips's least favourite part of the day, the time when, although the bulk of the work day had been successfully got through, often with surprising speed – oh look, it's twenty to twelve! oh look, it's five to two! – now that the end was in sight the clock mysteriously slowed down, so that the time between three thirty and five o'clock took what felt like six or seven hours, until 5.01, when the twenty-nine minutes until official going-home time at five thirty rocketed past.

It always takes Mr Phillips a few moments to adjust when he comes out of a cinema into the daylight. The feeling is voluptuous, sinful. He stands blinking and momentarily at a loss as to what he should do until it is time to go home. The thought of going back and waiting for Mrs Phillips to return from her lessons, which she would do at around five, appears in the distant wings of Mr Phillips's mind. She would come in, he would tell her what had happened. He catches a glimpse of the idea in the mental equivalent of peripheral vision and the notion scuttles back out of sight.

While still in the grip of his post-cinema daze, Mr Phillips comes to the end of the street and steps into the roadway without, it has to be admitted, looking left or right. A big white van swerves and comes to a stop about a foot away from him, so that he is looking straight into the face of its driver, which is first pale and then red. If the driver had reacted say .01 of a second more slowly Mr Phillips would have been run over. As part of Mr Phillips's mind is registering this fact, another part is noting that this vehicle was bound to have been a white van. In London, it always is. It must be either because (a), the vans tended to belong to self-employed small businessmen, who as a type were noted for being aggressive, impatient, right wing, unashamed about tactics of late payment and intimidation; (b), the vans tended to be driven by men working for large companies in some delivery and/or menial capacity, and so because the drivers had no stake in the vans they drove them aggressively, intimidatingly, recklessly, heedless of the full insured capital value; (c), there was something about white vans that made the people who drove them become irrationally aggressive – i.e., white vans made drivers go insane; (d), there was something about white vans that made aggressive men want to drive them – i.e., only people who were already insane drove white vans.

This particular white van driver winds down his window. Mr Phillips, unsure whether to go backwards or forwards across the road, sees that the man is showing no signs of climbing down out of the van and thumping him. So he continues across the street. As he does so the van driver leans out of his window. Here we go, thinks Mr Phillips.

'Tired of living, cunt?' asks the man in a neutral voice. He doesn't wait for a reply.

Across the road, under the lee of a theatre's stage door, a man is juggling three – no, four – fire torches. A small crowd has accumulated. They don't seem to be spectators so much as people who for the moment aren't doing anything else. The juggler's face is a distinctive dark brown colour, as if he has spent weeks and weeks out in the sun, and Mr Phillips has the feeling that he has seen him somewhere before. Of course: practising this very morning in Battersea Park. The man now picks up a fifth fire torch from the brazier in front of him. This, juggling with five torches, Mr Phillips knows is astoundingly difficult. The man, older than he looks at first glance – late thirties, perhaps – has a rapt, vacant look for the next thirty seconds or so, as the whirling torches pirouette in mid-air. Then he catches them, more clumsily than he juggled them, puts three of them back in the rack, and slowly, in a much more languorous and lingering way than the businesslike arts of fellation that Mr Phillips has just been watching, puts the other two, one after another, into his throat. When he takes them out they are extinguished. Mr Phillips notices that his erection has gone away. A member of the audience steps forward and drops a coin into the upside-down hat at the juggling fire-eater's feet.

It comes to Mr Phillips that he could set up in business on his own. The words arrive as a sentence, fully formed: 'I could set up on my own.' At the same time, it is unclear what precisely that means. He can hardly rent a shop and say 'Redundant fiftysomething accountant setting out on his own. Watch out, world.' He would need something specific to offer in the line of goods and services.

One thing would be to help people with their Income Tax returns and Value Added Tax obligations, or even give tentative savings and investment advice, though before he did that he would have somewhere to acquire a new manner and body language, since you would have to be very credulous to take advice about money from someone so obviously not thriving in his own personal finances. He would have to get a new wardrobe, new suits at the very least, a more modern haircut, office furniture that was either challengingly and interestingly contemporary or reassuringly old, a computer, even a new way of talking – avuncular, doctorly. The Revenue aren't as bad as people say, honestly, Mrs Wilson. Customs and Excise love a good joke, Mr Hart. Don't worry, Mr Stavros – bankruptcy means never having to say you're sorry.

He would be able to help small traders with their VAT, even though he thinks the name is very unfair, since it isn't a tax that adds value at all, but simply an extra sum the customers have to pay – a better name would be TAT, Tax Added Tax. If Mr Phillips sets up on his own he will have to charge and collect VAT and will therefore become what in the Bible is called a publican. St Matthew talks about someone being 'an heathen man and a publican', which at school Mr Phillips had thought was a bit harsh – what was so bad about running a pub? Then he found out. What's more, St Matthew had been one himself, a Jew raising money for the hated Roman Empire. Whereas Mr Phillips and his clients would merely be raising money for Government and for the EU so that people in Calabria could have tarmacked roads and French farmers could afford to keep their fields uneconomically small and make special cheese.

Of course there is always revenge. Revenge! He could sniff around for a gap in the catering services market, identify one – an under-performing staff canteen franchise, or a catastrophic outbreak of food poisoning from football match burgers – go to the bank or much more glamorously to a venture capital company, raise the money, make the pitch, win the contract, bid for other contracts, win them, exceed all expectations and industry standards, float the company on the stock market, make a packet, expand aggressively, seek out and destroy the competition while taking levels of service, customer satisfaction and percentage return on capital to unprecedented heights, finally close in on Wilkins and Co., strip them of their key customers, hire their talented employees, undercut their prices, in short drive them to the wall, then step in just before the receivers with a derisorily small but unrefusable cash offer. Mr Wilkins himself quivering on Phillips Limited's boardroom carpet, fourteen stone of jelly merely pretending to be a man. All the old management fired, or better still kept on at half their old pay, and made to attend regular seminars at which their faults are pointed out and enthusiastically discussed by younger but more senior colleagues; Mr Mill exposed as a drunkard and numerical dyslexic, his employment as head of department over Mr Phillips appearing in textbooks as a definitive example of the psychology of corporate incompetence.

Mr Phillips stops across the road from a squat church with a tall spire that looks out of proportion and a scruffy graveyard behind high, spiked black railings. A poster on them advertises Teatime Talks and underneath it, under the heading *All Religions Dip Their Buckets Into the Same River*, a talk for today, at 3 o'clock, on the subject of 'What We Can All Learn From Buddhism'. Mr Phillips goes through the open gate and takes the short gravelled path through the graveyard. He is momentarily startled when he glances to his right and sees what looks like a dead body lying on the grass. Then he realizes it is a tramp having a snooze. Balanced intact on the tramp's stomach is an open can of Tennents Super, ready for immediate swigging when he wakes up.

The church porch is suddenly and unexpectedly cool. In fact it's the least hot place Mr Phillips has been in all day. The noticeboard is fronted in green felt and has the words Holy Trinity written across the top in fading gilt. It holds announcements about drug rehabilitation, a flower arranging roster, a list of names in a prayer chain, whatever that is, and a notice of the sequence of services and evensongs, along with the liturgy to be used. To Mr Phillips, cradle though lapsed Catholic, these are an exotic touch, something he never got used to about the Church of England, where the language might be either rollingly archaic or as flatly modern as a leaflet from the Inland Revenue.

Churches don't mean much to Mr Phillips. He doesn't find anything odd about that. An extraterrestrial would look at the number and apparent importance of churches in Britain, calculate the resources that must have been devoted to building them, and come up with a hugely wrong estimate of their importance in the national life. Both the Phillips boys were brought up nominally Catholic as a way of getting into St Francis Xavier, the local not-bad Catholic school. Religion per se isn't something to which any of the family – certainly not Mrs Phillips, an unimpassioned but lifelong atheist – gives a great deal of thought.

The heavy, thick oak door into the church proper is half open, and Mr Phillips squeezes through into the main body of the building. Like all churches, presumably because they are always empty, it feels bigger on the inside than the out. Plain glass windows along both aisles admit some light but not much; the high fluorescent tubes add a sense of epileptic flicker but little else. Towards the altar, orange plastic stackable chairs – which is what the church has instead of pews – have been arranged in a semicircle for a dozen or so people to sit and listen to a man who sits opposite them. One of the people sitting in this half moon of chairs, a cross-looking middle aged woman wearing a duffle coat, turns and glares at Mr Phillips for three seconds until her expression suddenly switches to a full-wattage smile. She looks as if she has been appraising the likelihood that he is a burglar or beggar and has decided that he isn't. Then she turns back to the speaker. Luckily, at this range Mr Phillips can't hear what he is saying.

The main body of the nave is empty, with chairs stacked teeteringly high against the two walls. It creates a curious sense of exposure; there are no pews to duck into, no copies of the Alternative Service Book to pretend to read. The only distraction is provided by a table at the back of the church, strewn with pamphlets: *How to Pray, What Jesus Can Mean to You, Is There a Hole in Your Life*? There is a photocopied leaflet offering a history of the building for 10p and another providing a guided tour. Mr Phillips feels that having come into the church he cannot, especially now he has been spotted, simply turn on his heel and walk away, so he takes a copy of the 10p tour leaflet and pretends to look at the new stained glass window in the middle of the north wall. Its centrepiece is a joky version of Noah's Ark, with the patriarch afloat in his tiny boat behind a unicorn, a dinosaur and a sort of griffin. Someone paid for this to be done in 1962 by some artist Mr Phillips has never heard of. It is typical of the public art that seems to be scattered about London more or less randomly – the tiny blob-like Henry Moore sculpture just around the corner from Wilkins and Co., monuments to generals no one has ever heard of, all that. Meanwhile the city is inhabited by people 99.999 per cent of whom will never have a monument built to them, and who know it, and who repay the compliment by ignoring all the monuments and memorials to toffs and nobs and heroes and famous victories.

Mr Phillips is now within earshot of the talk.

'. . . so that there's a sense, a very real sense,' the earnest man in the centre of the group is saying, 'in which the idea of reincarnation is a Christian idea, the embodiment of those responsibilities to all living things that St Francis taught, and the idea of, you know, stewardship, so that if you go around thinking that cows and lizards and even, sort of, ants are people too, in a sense, then you won't sort of step on them or whatever it is.'

This appears to have been the climactic part of his talk. He stops speaking, slumps back into his seat and looks around the group with a bright expression. There is a silence and a shuffling. Mr Phillips's least favourite part of any discussion or talk or meeting, from the PTA at St Francis Xavier's to the weekly accounts overview session at Wilkins and Co., is precisely this point, when people look at their shoes or rearrange their paperwork and pray that someone will say something, ask something, do something. It is as if everyone in the room simultaneously and immediately becomes intensely self-conscious. As he stands still, and the chill of the stone floor begins to seep up through his shoes, he is aware of how much his feet hurt, a stinging ache that he hasn't felt for years.

'Niceness is so important, isn't it?' says the woman who glared at Mr Phillips. She has a bright, well-bred, carrying voice. There is not quite a murmur of agreement, but a shuffling and grunting and grinning. The man who gave the talk nods enthusiastically.

'That's so true,' he says. But this intervention hasn't been pitched at the right level and the silence descends again. Mr Phillips feels pinned down as if by a sniper, since if he begins walking his echoing footfall will be by far the loudest noise in the church. The pause is broken by a balding man in a T-shirt, who says in a flat and oddly loud voice, as if he were wearing a pair of earphones and talking at the same time:

'The thing I don't understand is, you improve your karma by acting ethically, yes?'

The talk-giver, with what looks like artificial calm, says:

'We would perhaps say not that you improve your karma but that in a very real sense you *are* it.'

'Fine, fine. So we behave well and move up the reincarnation ladder. Be nice to your granny and go up three notches. Be nasty to babies and dogs and move down five notches. Move down enough notches and you're reborn as a moose or a dragonfly or whatever. Finally you end up as a cockroach. And then you begin to move back up the ladder so that you're reborn as a human being. Right? That's the general idea?'

The other man seems less alarmed now. He spreads his hands and says:

'Very *very* broadly speaking. I'd suggest that . . .'

'OK, OK,' goes on the flat-voiced man. 'So let's say you're nasty to everyone, you don't pay your TV licence fee or return your library books, and you're reborn as a crocodile. You've been a bad boy so now you're a crocodile. There you are in your creek in the Upper Limpopo or whatever. Now here's my question: how do you improve your karma? How do you behave well? What does an ethical crocodile look like?'

There is a loud pause. People seem embarrassed but interested. There is also, suddenly, the risk of a scene, and that is one of Mr Phillips's least favourite things. That dislike does seem to be genetic, a horror of raised voices and raised blood pressure that he without question inherited from his father and mother. 'A man who loses his temper is a ridiculous man,' his father would say, and indeed he never publicly lost his temper, merely turning quiet and pale and clenching his teeth and being unable to prevent a reedy, shaky edge coming into his voice, when he was angry – which he often was, especially at public slights on the part of people who were supposed to be helping or serving or looking after him, car park attendants and cinema ushers and, when he was in hospital for a prostate operation a year before he died, the nurses and caterers, although not the doctors, since their status was superior to his and so the transaction worked in a different way. His anxieties were to do with status and the respect he felt should be accorded to him but wasn't. All these people should be giving it to him, in the form of prompt, respectful, attentive help, and if they didn't he would become angry, would turn in on himself, and would sit silently and furiously brooding while more vociferous complainers would speak and get attention or amends. This in turn would make

179

his mute sulking rage, his silent, passive temper tantrum, all the worse.

Mr Phillips's mother, on the other hand, seemed not to have a temper at all, although she would sometimes go quiet and depressed, often in response to her husband's sulk – it was as if she caught the feeling from him, though in a milder form. They shared a horror of altercations, public displays of crossness, all forms of ruction, and so did their son, who is beginning to wish that he wasn't where he is, as the earnest man tries to gather himself and counter-attack.

'Well,' the talk-giver says. This gets the other man going again.

'What about an ant? Or a praying mantis? Or a piranha? Or a virus? What's a well-behaved flu virus do so that it can be reborn as an amoeba or a protozoon? How does a wasp improve its karma?'

'Well,' says the other man again. A youngish woman who had not spoken up before suddenly says in a loud, posh, mad voice:

'Jesus died for your sins. Do you understand that? He died for your sins.'

'But St Francis would never –'

'I mean, if you're just going around stinging people, and that's your actual *job* –'

'The sacrifice that He made for *you* –'

'. . . we're getting a bit away from the –'

'. . . simple question –'

'. . . in between a thief and a murderer –'

'. . . more a sort of metaphor thingy –'

'. . . crocodile-skin handbags –'

'. . . Our Saviour, mine and yours –'

'. . . difference of emphasis.'

Four or five people are now talking at once. From being shy or cowed they are now being voluble and, to varying extents, cross.

'Vicarious suffering! Vicarious suffering!' shouts the posh, loud, mad one in an even louder, madder voice.

Mr Phillips realizes that at least some of these people know each other and have had this argument, or at least a version of it, before. He decides to seize the opportunity to make a bid for freedom. Without moving too quickly, he starts walking towards the exit. As he gets to the heavy door and pulls it towards him, the man with the flat voice sees him and calls out:

'Oi! Where do you think you're going?'

At least half the group burst into approving, jeering, raucous laughter, and that is the last sound Mr Phillips hears as he slips out into the porch. In the churchyard the tramp does not seem to have moved at all, but the can of lager that was balanced on his stomach is no longer there.

What do you call a man with a seagull on his head? Cliff. What do you call a man with a spade in his head? Doug. What do you call a man with no arms and no legs in the ocean? Bob. What do you call a man with ten rabbits up his bum? Warren.

Mr Phillips is lying face down on the floor of Barclays Bank. His arms are spread above and on either side of his head, and his jacket has ridden up and bunched so that it feels as if his circulation is being cut off around his shoulders. Also it is very hot. But Mr Phillips does not want to adjust his position and make himself more comfortable, because four men with shotguns have taken over the bank and it is on their orders that he is lying on the floor looking at the Barclays carpet and trying to keep calm. When the men communicate they do so by shouting and their threats are easy to believe. They have said that they will blow the fucking head off any fucker who moves.

Funnily enough, Mr Phillips saw the men come into the bank just as he noticed a sign saying 'No Crash Helmets Please'. About two seconds later four men wearing jeans, windcheaters and crash helmets walked into the bank, and there was a split second in which Mr Phillips was noticing and remarking on the coincidence – oh look, there are men in crash helmets, who I don't suppose will know they're not meant to come in here dressed like that – before the men started shouting commands and making everyone lie on the floor. One of the crash helmets then picked a middle aged woman in a perm up off the floor and held what appeared to be a sawn-off shotgun, an object about a foot and a half long with a double barrel, at her head. He told the cashiers that if they did not buzz him through to their part of the bank, behind the glass partition, he would blow her face off. So the cashiers buzzed him and one of his companions through while the other two robbers stayed outside and patrolled the banking hall.

How many hairdressers does it take to change a light bulb? Five – one to change the bulb, four to stand around saying 'Super, Gary.' How many yuppies does it take to change a light bulb? Two – one to change the bulb, one to organize a skip. How many therapists does it take to change a light bulb? None – the light bulb can change itself, but only if it *wants* to. How many feminists does it take to change a light bulb? One – and it's not funny. How many feminists does it take to change a light bulb? Two – one to change the bulb, the other to suck your cock.

That was one of Martin's.

It is all Mr Phillips's fault that he was caught in here. He had not really needed to come into the bank at all. In fact, all day, on and off, he has been deliberately not-thinking about going to the bank and asking for an up-to-date statement of his financial position, checking his balance, which is about £500, and his savings account, which is about £3000, before he gets his three months' tax free redundancy, which would come to about £8000. But this was something he simply could not face doing, so he had not-thought about it until what seemed at first to be a happy accident had happened.

Mr Phillips had come out of the church and wandered down to Shaftesbury Avenue. As the day went on London seemed to be getting busier and busier – more people, more rushing about, more cars, more tourists, more cycle couriers and motor-cycle messengers, more red buses and black taxis and angry white vans, more coaches and coach parties and more girls and more men carrying things and in a hurry. It was ever so slightly less warm than it had been, at least on the side of the road that wasn't in the direct sun. Mr Phillips could feel the cold patches on his back where the shirt had soaked up sweat. He knew that his feet would by now be humming up a storm.

A man came up Shaftesbury Avenue leading a group of Asian tourists who had clearly just come out of a matinée of *Les Misérables*. They were clutching programmes. The guide was holding up a bright orange umbrella and kept pivoting to check that his flock was still there behind him. Then a cyclist shot past Mr Phillips where he stood, swerved between a pair of European-looking tourists and a young man carrying a Tower Records bag, hopped in the air as his bike went over the kerb, cut up a taxi and hurtled over a pedestrian crossing before mounting the pavement and setting off towards Piccadilly Circus.

It was nearly four. Mr Phillips had to use up another two and a half hours before he could plausibly arrive home. It occurred to him for a brief, mad moment that he could even walk the distance . . . but that would be daft, he was tired enough as it was. A couple of hours more walking would finish him off.

He crossed the road and began walking towards Piccadilly, in the wake of the demon cyclist. About fifty yards along a temporary bus stop had been erected, compensating for the fact that the permanent bus stop was submerged under a pile of scaffolding where something was being built or demolished or painted or cleaned. As he walked up to the stop, a Routemaster bus, spewing thick black diesel fumes, pulled up beside him and twenty or thirty people began to get off, the younger and nimbler of them not waiting for the bus to stop but hopping off and hitting the ground running. The first of them, a young black man, jumped off with a dancer's wide leap, buckled for a moment with the effort of adjusting his momentum as he hit the ground, and then jogged off towards Chinatown.

When he had had things to do Mr Phillips had not noticed how busy, how urgent, everybody in the city seemed.

Mr Phillips got on the bus. He went upstairs to the top deck and sat down at the front.

This bus went through all the glamorous parts of London. First it went down past the Trocadero, down Haymarket, then back up Regent Street to Piccadilly, then along past the Royal Academy, past the Ritz, past Green Park, round Hyde Park Corner, and along Knightsbridge. By and large these were all parts of London that Mr Phillips never visited. They belonged to other kinds of people. The feeling of wealth and prosperity was thickly present in all these places, and it made Mr Phillips wonder what the city would look like if, instead of bricks and mortar, concrete and cement, buildings were made out of piles of stacked cash, wadded and glued together into bricks. A house out in Leytonstone would be say eight foot high, a sort of wattle hut made out of fivers, whereas one in Knightsbridge would be a skyscraper of £20 notes. And the people, too: if they were nothing more than their total capital value they would vary from tiny bunches, hardly visible, of rolled up notes, to towers thousands of feet tall, stretching up into the clouds, causing trouble for air traffic control and weather balloons, vulnerable to lightning. Mr Phillips himself would be a respectable man-sized pile of cash, if you counted the unmortgaged part of 27 Wellesley Crescent, though he would soon start shrinking fast. If you excluded the house, the assets held jointly with Mrs Phillips and the ones in her name, and deducted debts such as the unpaid part of the mortgage, he would be much less healthy – barely a briefcaseful.

Mr Phillips often thinks about people's time and what it costs. The ideal is the taxi meter, ticking away to show how much the customer is spending, every penny accounted for and all above board. The red numerals travelling in one direction only. Everyone should have a little meter on them, in Mr Phillips's view – lawyers in court, politicians on the television; a special lightweight one for footballers and athletes; bus drivers, housewives, Mrs Phillips during her piano lessons and Mr Phillips himself at the office. Only the off duty and the unemployed would be exempt; perhaps they would wear meters that had been switched off, or meters stuck on their last reading. Or should they show average earnings across time, so that even people on unemployment would tick slowly along? The whole point would be the way people chug along at different rates: Mr Mill, who cost £45,000 a year, would clock along at 45,000 divided by 250 (working days per year) divided by 7 (working hours per working day) = £25.71 per hour, whereas the beloved and much fancied Karen would tick along at £18,000 divided by 250 (working days per year) divided by 7 (working hours per working day) = £ 10.29 per hour, with everyone else in the office, from Eric the charismatic head of the post room to Mr Wilkins himself, who was sighted by someone in accounts about twice a year, ticking away at their own personal rates, the whole process giving an added point or edge to all interpersonal transactions in the office, something to notice and think about, though it would no doubt become quickly invisible as everyone got used to it, as everyone always does. (That of course would happen even if little green men landed and were on the nine o'clock news – after a few weeks' initial excitement humanity would go back to business as usual.)

The system could get elaborate. For instance, actors could have to wear two meters, one showing their rate and the other the rate of the characters they were playing, indicated perhaps by green numerals as opposed to red ones. You would see an actor playing one part, the paterfamilias in an historical drama, with trademark mutton chop whiskers, and then not see him for months or even a year or two until he turned up again as the butler in an advertisement for vintage port, and you'd realize from looking at his meter, still stuck at the figure it had been on at the end of the drama series, that he'd been 'resting' in the interim. Sometimes a famous and highly paid actor would be playing a penniless waif, and the difference between the two meters would become horribly distracting. Musicians would tick away as they played on *Top of the Pops*, newsreaders and politicians while they talked, beggars as they sat on the street, bus drivers, nurses, waiters, yellow-hat construction workers, everyone. The meters would have different settings to reflect earnings this day, earnings this task, and lifetime earnings. The Prime Minister was paid £57,018, in addition of course to his salary as an MP, but how much he ticked away at per hour would depend on whether you thought he was on duty all the time, whether his holidays were proper holidays etc. The President of the USA was paid about £125,000 and the same thing applied.

Mr Phillips's bus emerged from Hyde Park Corner and began heading down Knightsbridge. The traffic bottlenecked momentarily to squeeze past a BMW that had been stopped by a police motorcyclist. The policeman was talking to the driver, a tall black man wearing sunglasses.

And now, as the bus went past Harrods, Mr Phillips, who

had been looking at people in the street in an idle, incurious way, felt a jolt of surprised excitement. He had spotted her! It was Clarissa Colingford, sure as eggs were eggs, the TV person he had been thinking and indeed masturbating about on and off for some months. She was crossing the street, coming out of a clothes shop with a parcel labelled Chez Guevara under her arm, at some speed, tripping along at a near-run, looking pretty, busy, preoccupied. She was shorter than she seemed on TV and less lifelike – less like herself than like the generic idea of a thin, youngish, blonde woman in expensive clothes. In fact if Mr Phillips had seen her in real life first he might well have been inoculated against her. But he hadn't and he wasn't and, deeply curious to get a second look, he got off the bus at the next stop, doubled back, picked up her trail further along Knightsbridge, becoming a stalker or private detective for all of about three minutes, until she had suddenly swerved to one side and gone into the bank, a branch of the very same bank that Mr Phillips himself patronized.

A real man shoots his own dog. Mr Phillips decided to be a man: he would go in, draw some cash and request a full statement sent to his home address. If he happened to bump into Clarissa Colingford, their hands brushing together as they simultaneously reached for a deposit slip, no please after you, no I insist, took me a moment to find them it's not my usual branch, yes South London, oh do you how interesting, yes a cup of coffee would be delightful . . . well, that would just be one of those freak coincidences. Which is how Mr Phillips came to be lying face down on the floor of this bank, ten feet away from Clarissa Colingford, at the business end of a sawn-off shotgun. It was just one of those things.

At this range he can see that it's some outfit she has on. Her thin pale-brown shirt looks as if it were made out of chamois leather, and her thin-looking cream trousers unfortunately seem likely to pick up all kinds of dirts and smears from the Barclays carpet. From this distance she is more like she is on TV than at medium range. She has the same sense of invisible shine and of being almost too good to be true, though she is skinnier than she seems on television, by about ten pounds, which makes her seem more nervous, less voluptuous, but immediately wantable. She looks, not sweaty, but as if you might, if you got up very close to her, see a faint clamminess at the base of her neck, in the crook of her elbow, her perfume enhanced by her body heat. Mr Phillips feels that he is very much in love.

This carpet however has Mr Phillips worried. Once you are pressed out cruciform on any floor surface – prostrated, they would say in church, in the position priests used to adopt when being ordained – you begin to think about what else has been on that floor before you. In the case of a much trodden-on urban bank carpet there is the question of dog shit on people's shoes. Also pigeon shit, urine, rubbish, spilt things; but mainly dog shit. It would be picked up, brought here, and then trodden into the carpet which was now an inch from Mr Phillips's nose, a pale blue flooring made out of some industrial substance with a tight knobbly weave, the better to capture millions of tiny molecules of transported dog excrement, the sort that made children blind if they ate it. Why would they eat it, you might well ask, to which the answer was, accidents do happen.

Mr Phillips once went through a phase of being worried about dog shit in London's parks, on behalf of the children. For instance that Martin would kick the football through some dog shit, pick the ball up without noticing, rub his eyes or polish an apple with the contaminated hand, and become sick. It was something to do with worms. Then the worries had gone away, apparently of their own accord. Now they have come back again. It is as if he can see tiny particles of dog shit everywhere he looks.

Clarissa Colingford had come into the bank and gone straight over to the cashpoint machine. Or not quite straight over; she had stood around looking vague for a moment or two and then gone to stand behind a hugely fat man who was having tremendous difficulty inserting his card into the automatic teller. Mr Phillips knew this fine art well and knew that it was all a matter of timing, but this man's stiff, jabbing action – and who knew whether the card was even the right way round! – and the quiet mechanical crunch of the card being rejected made something obscene out of his failure to insert it. Finally Clarissa Colingford stepped in, coming up beside the man and with the sweetest expression saying, 'May I?'

The big man handed her the card and she slipped it into the purring machine at the first attempt.

'Well, thanks,' he said. She just smiled, as if saying anything might compromise his maleness, and stood back as he hunched scowling over the console. Mr Phillips felt intensely jealous. He lurched to one side before he was caught eavesdropping and moved to the counter where you filled in slips, did sums, and took leaflets. It was there that he was standing when the robbers burst into the bank.

Of course she could have used the cashpoint outside if it was only cash she wanted. Mr Phillips suspects that he knows the reason why she didn't. This Knightsbridge cashpoint can be relied on to have at least one beggar sitting or standing beside it, plaintively (usually) or aggressively (occasionally) asking for money, usually by saying, 'Spare change please?' Today there was a woman, probably in her thirties but looking ten years older, sitting half rolled-up in too many clothes for the weather – heavy trousers, two or three shirts, a coat, a bobble hat, with a couple of plastic bags strewn around her. She looked pitiful, but in Mr Phillips's experience that doesn't always make you want to give someone money. This beside-the-cashpoint spot must be prime territory; Mr Phillips wondered if beggars took turns occupying it. To Mr Phillips's mind there was something hard to ignore about the juxtaposition of someone asking for money, needing it desperately even, and the money that the machine was vomiting or belching out to people who asked for it. It was as if there was a right way and a wrong way of asking for money: sit on the pavement and ask your fellow humans and you'll be refused, stand up and ask a machine and you can have as much as you want.

Mr Phillips sometimes feels a wave of anger or revulsion as he walks past a beggar. When he gives one money, usually 50p since they aren't useful for parking meters, the emotion he feels is not primarily towards the beggar but towards himself, a warm glow of philanthropic self-congratulation. Similarly, the other feelings are directed at himself too, at his ungenerosity and ability to harden his own heart. It is this that makes people hate beggars, for what they make you do to them – since no one can give money to every beggar he sees, the existence of beggars turns everybody into the kind of person who walks past beggars. Hard to forgive them that.

The men who are robbing the bank are not asking for money so much as simply taking it, and taking their time about doing it too, in Mr Phillips's view. Though admittedly his ability to judge how much time has passed is probably not at its best. It feels like twenty minutes but is probably more like two. This would be something to talk about when he got home – though if he does he will have to say where he's been, and what he was doing in Knightsbridge at four in the afternoon, which is something he doesn't particularly feel like doing. This is another subject he prefers to not-think about.

'Check that one,' shouts one of the men behind the counter. Mr Phillips doesn't want to look and see what is going on but can guess that it probably involves stashing bags full of cash. The curious thing is that because the robbers shout all the time – which Mr Phillips knows from watching *Crimewatch UK* is a trick to make it hard for people to identify their voices or accents – they sound a little like the head of department Mr Phillips had had at Grimshaw's, a man called or rather nicknamed Knobber. He had shouted all the time too and had been able to call on a bottomless source of seemingly unfeigned anger. He once described his department's performance in preparing at twenty-four hours' notice for an audit as the worst day in the history of the accountancy profession.

Why are there no aspirin in the jungle? Paracetamol. (Parrots eat 'em all.) Have you ever seen a bunny with its nose all runny, don't say it's funny 'cos it's snot. What do you get if you cross a nun with an apple? A computer that won't go down on you. Have you heard about the evil dyslexic? He sold his soul to Santa. Have you heard about the agnostic insomniac dyslexic? He lay awake all night wondering if there was a Dog. Why did the chicken kill itself? To get to the other side.

This is the closest Mr Phillips has ever been to actual violence in his whole adult life, excluding the occasional scuffle in the street, not that he's taken part in one – God forbid – but because he occasionally sees them out of a car or a train window. Mr Phillips must have witnessed many thousands of violent incidents, shootings and explosions and stabbings and abductions and rapes and fist fights and drive-by machine-gunnings, and assassination style head shots and Saturday Night Special shootings, and cars blown up by shoulder fired rocket launchers, and rooms systematically cleared by grenades followed by machine-gun fire, and petrol stations blown up by deliberately dropped cigarette lighters, but all of these were on television (or occasionally at the movies). The last proper stand-up fist fight he saw was nineteen years ago, when he spent six months commuting to the plant in Banbury, a few years after he started at Wilkins and Co. A foreman from Newcastle had accused a fitter from London, a Cockney wide boy whom nobody much liked – the plant was the first place Mr Phillips had realized how much 'Cockneys', as all Londoners were called, were disliked – of being a thief. Twenty pounds, then quite a lot of money, had gone missing from the Geordie's locker. The Geordie had won by making the Cockney's nose bleed so much that the fight had to stop so that he could go and get it looked at in Casualty. There was no more thieving, though no one ever found out who had stolen the money. As would happen in a film, the two men later became inseparably fast friends.

The two robbers in the front part of the bank are prowling around the room keeping order. Occasionally one or other of them stands so close to him that Mr Phillips gets a good view of his footwear. One of them has on a pair of expensive-looking new trainers, one of the brands that children wear and now, these days, rob and murder to own. The other has on an old pair of tennis shoes that have a slight and very incongruous air of raffishness – the kind of shoes a stockbroker with two homes might wear in the country at weekends, on one of the days he isn't bothering to shave. Both of them wear jeans.

About a dozen customers are in the bank. Mr Phillips wonders how many of them have recognized Clarissa Colingford and whether any of them feels, not the same way that he does, since that would be impossible, but something, however faintly, similar. Three or four of the customers are men: there are two businessmen, and a scruffy youth who fifteen years ago would have been a punk. Luckily, none of the women has children in tow. Perhaps that is an accident or perhaps the robbers have been careful about their timing.

There must be a lot of detail to have to think about, being a bank robber. It would seem like a job for the headstrong and reckless but there must be a great deal of planning in it too. It would attract a curious type of person, willing to risk their own lives and threaten other people's but also prepared to take pains over things like escape routes, what kind of getaway car to use, how to dodge the traffic, best time to rob the bank, how long it would take the police to get there and so on. It wouldn't be the sort of thing where you had a few beers and were suddenly seized with the need to put a helmet on, grab a sawn-off, and go rob a bank.

The rewards must justify the risks. That stood to reason. Enough robbers must do well enough to keep the profession alive. But how well was well enough? It must be hard to be precise about robbers' average wages. Some would do well, some less well, and since doing less well involved spending years in prison there would be no sensible way of averaging them out. How did you compare a year in which you cleared £100,000 (and that free of tax) and took the whole family to Barbados to one in which you got sent to prison for a decade?

But presumably if he were to tell the armed robbers that he has worked in an office for more than a quarter of a century, earning a top salary of £32,000, and had just been made redundant, they would think that was hilarious. In fact, if you spent eight hours a day for thirty years in an office that was the same as spending ten years in jail for twenty-four hours a day – and it was an unlucky bank robber who actually spent ten years in the slammer, since you always served a good bit less than you were sentenced for, and in jail you could read books, do a degree, that sort of thing. There would be no shortage of time spent doing nothing.

In films there were people in prison who controlled huge criminal syndicates from the comfort and safety of their own cells. Tell Levinsky if he comes back and asks nicely, plus gives us 90 per cent of the gross, I won't chop his dick off and stick it in his mouth, growls Mr Phillips the mob boss to his quailing deputy, who has brought the twice-weekly delivery of Krug and sevruga in a Harrods bag, right under the noses of the bribed and terrified warders. Tell that kid in Streatham he needs to show a little more respect. Nothing too heavy – break his arms, torch his Beamer. You OK Joe, you look a little pale. Maybe you're not eating right. Or maybe you're staying up too late fucking that little piece of totty you're running on the side. Yeah that's right I hear things, you should show your wife a little more respect. A man who doesn't spend time with his family is not a real man. How are Janie and the kids, I hear Luigi got into St Paul's, you must be very proud. A model prisoner, revered by his fellow inmates in the lax regime of the Open Prison, gracefully accepting their unsolicited gifts of cigarettes and phone cards.

Apparently armed robbers were looked up to in prison. Mr Phillips has read that somewhere. Sex criminals were the lowest form of life, whereas armed robbers were the aristocrats.

How do you tell the difference between a stoat and a weasel? One's weasily recognizable, the other's stotally different. What do you call a man with no arms and no legs crawling through a forest? Russell. What do you say to a woman with two black eyes? Nothing, you've told her twice already. Martin again. Perhaps he should tell that one to the robbers. It might be their kind of joke.

Mr Phillips can hear a woman crying, about fifteen feet away from where he is lying. It is a choking, moaning sort of cry, as if she were making every effort to minimize the amount of noise – which of course makes things worse. Mr Phillips could remember his own efforts not to cry at his father's funeral, and the feeling that his chest would crack open; as if he were struggling to contain volcanic forces. The effort made his shoulders jerk and his chin wobble, and strangled choking sounds came out of his mouth. In those days men did not cry at funerals. The feat of suppression involved was in its way as wild and violent as any open grief.

His father once, when Mr Phillips, aged about nine, fell and cut his knee on gravel – he can no longer remember where, only his father's words stay with him – told him to stop crying, that it made him look like a girl. That happened over forty years ago, and it is still one of Mr Phillips's most vivid memories. It is as if the stream of tears was at that moment diverted underground and has not been seen properly above the surface since. In the meantime it went sloshing around out of sight like the run-off from a broken water main coursing through the foundations of a house. In childhood, as far as he can remember, crying had inside it the idea that this feeling would go on for ever – that the pain, whatever it was, that was causing you to cry was infinite and would possess you for ever. Or you would live inside it for ever. Now he sees it as the first vague intimation of what death would be like – to be in the same state without end.

Mrs Phillips cries easily at films and more rarely at music, but she isn't as much of a crier as Mr Phillips would have been if he had been a woman, or so he feels. She does not shake or heave. Tears simply begin to appear in her eyes and waterfall down her face, accompanied by sniffles. It is like a spring or a well or some other non-volcanic phenomenon. Both Martin and Thomas have inherited this ability, which Mr Phillips has been at pains not to discourage. No doubt part of the reason this woman is struggling is the effort involved in crying when you are lying spreadeagled face down on the floor. Mr Phillips has not tried that and has no plans to.

Death is another subject Mr Phillips exerts himself, not always successfully, to not-think about. He has got to the stage when it only enters his mind when someone he knows died –

Betty his first-ever secretary of cancer last year, Finker his friend from accounting school of a heart attack at Christmas, Mr Elton, Thomas's favourite football teacher in a car crash in January, were the most recent. These deaths always bring a wave of anxiety and of me-too, me-next, what-will-it-be-like thoughts. One of Mr Phillips's least favourite reveries involves the idea of lying in a hospital listening to a beeping monitor, wondering if this time would be It. When you are young sex is It, when you are older death is.

Not so much being dead as dying is what frightens Mr Phillips. This is a question which divides people, and he knows the arguments for the other point of view, not least because Mrs Phillips subscribes to them.

'The awfulness of nothing. To lose all this,' she explained. They were sitting in their kitchen, which was throbbing with the noise of moronic neighbours revving their car engines as per their Saturday norm, but even so Mr Phillips knew what she meant.

None the less, he doesn't see it that way. Not being here is in itself nothing to fear. The moment of transition, though – the moment of breaking through the veil of being-here and going through to notness, which presumably involves a terrible rending moment in which you realize what is happening, have full consciousness of what you are going through – now *that* seems to be worth fearing. If he could have a written guarantee from the responsible parties that death would be something he wouldn't notice – here one moment, gone the next, with no lived transition – he would feel perfectly sanguine, even gung-ho, about the whole business. But the thought that you would be aware of what was going on as you died implied that somewhere in his future was a moment of the purest terror, terror at 200 proof, so that you could have a small taste of the fear every time you let your mind touch on the subject, even for a second or two.

Today, lying here on the floor of the bank, must be the closest Mr Phillips had been to death for many years – perhaps the closest since his friend Tony Wilson, who moved to Dorset to run a minicab company and whom he hadn't seen for fifteen years, had crashed their car on the way back from a wedding in Suffolk. Tony was drunk – not paralytic, but tipsy. He had taken a corner too fast, skidded, and gone into a ditch about ten feet from a concrete drainage pipe. If they had hit the pipe they would have been dead.

'You're very lucky young men,' the policemen had told them.

'If we'd been that lucky what were we doing in the fucking ditch in the first place?' Tony said. He knew that he was going to lose his licence anyway.

Mrs Phillips, who had been at home because she was eight and a half months pregnant with Martin and couldn't face the round-trip drive to East Anglia, had forbidden her husband from ever travelling in a car driven by Tony again. That was a quarter of a century ago. Since then the nearest Mr Phillips has come to death is through the usual risks to do with strokes and heart attacks and haemorrhages, the things which can jump up and whack you, take you at any moment, as well as the longer-term, more stealthy killers, the ones that creep up on you from behind and kidnap you into the treeless country of terminal illness – the cancers, the degenerative diseases. In that sense he has lived with the same proximity to death as any other sedentary man in his fifties with a white collar job, the kind of intimacy you could have with an acquaintance who might drop in at any moment but who you would probably at the same time have no reason to expect on this particular day, or on any other day for a little while yet.

This raises the question of how likely death is, on any particular day. It came up one morning a few months ago, when they were all sitting around before the monthly progress meeting of the Accounts Department.

'Hang on a minute,' said Abbot, the youngest of them. 'The odds against winning the Lottery are fourteen million to one, right?'

'The odds against winning the jackpot,' said Monroe in his Aberdonian voice. 'Six divided by forty nine times five divided by forty eight times four divided by forty seven times three divided by forty six times two divided by forty five times one divided by forty four, which is 0.00000007151 or one in 13,983,816, usually referred to as one in fourteen million. So if the prize is greater than fourteen million quid it becomes a rational bet as supposed to just a stupidity tax.'

'Assuming all the money goes to only one winner, which you can't assume,' said somebody else.

'Fourteen million to one that you'll get all six numbers right,' said Monroe. 'There is however another risk here which affects the likelihood of winning. Does anybody want to tell me what it is?'

Mr Phillips, who knew the answer because he had heard Monroe on the subject before, kept silent so as not to spoil his fun.

'No takers. All right. The additional factor that needs to be taken into consideration is the chance of being dead by the time the Lottery results arrive – since, obviously, the chance of dying in any given week is much, much higher than that of winning the Lottery.'

There was a pause, the sound of six accountants sizing up a mathematical problem in their heads.

'What's the death rate? How many people die every week?' said Austen.

'According to the relevant Government agencies,' said Monroe, 'the population of England at the time of the last estimate was 49,300,000. The previous year, deaths totalled 526,650. The death rate per week was therefore 10,128, rounded up to the nearest cadaver. Using these data we find that for an Englishman the chance of dying in any given week is therefore 0.0002054, or one in 4880.'

'So your chance of winning the Lottery', said Abbot at his calculator, 'is, er, 2873 times worse than your chance of being dead by the time of the National Lottery draw.'

'But we're assuming you buy the ticket at the start of the

week,' Monroe went on. 'In other words, if you buy your ticket at the start of the week and hold it until the draw, your chance of being dead by the time of the result is much better than your chance of winning. But most people don't buy the ticket on Sunday, they buy it in the middle of the week before the draw, and so their odds are better. If you buy your ticket at four o'clock on Friday afternoon your chance of not being dead before the result must be significantly improved.'

They were already doing the sums.

'Assuming the deaths are spread evenly over the calendar –'

– which Mr Phillips didn't feel you could assume. Surely more people died in winter and at weekends, of drinking and fighting and the stress of being cooped up with their families and so on? But he didn't say anything –

'That means that the chance of dying, for a random member of the population, is 0.0107 per year, or 0.0000293 per day, or 0.00000122 per hour, or 0.0000000203 per minute. In other words each of us has a 1 in 49,200,000 chance of dying in any given minute. So in order for the probability of winning the jackpot to be greater than the chance of being dead by the time of the draw one would have to bet no earlier than', Monroe tapped some figures into his Psion Organiser, 'three and a half minutes before the draw.'

'Christ,' said someone.

'But that's averaging the risk out,' Monroe continued. 'Obviously a nineteen-year-old girl who doesn't drink, doesn't smoke, has no familial history of anything and whose great-grandmother is still alive at the age of 102 is more likely not to be dead than a sixty-year-old chain-smoking alcoholic with a Private Pilot's licence. We'd need to get hold of some proper actuarial tables,' he concluded, giving the word 'proper' a discreet but very Scottish emphasis. At that point Mr Mill the useless departmental head came into the room, the conversation petered out and the meeting began instead.

Monroe, however, did not forget. About two weeks later a notice appeared on the board in the company canteen saying ATTENTION LOTTERY GAMBLERS, and below giving a breakdown, along the lines discussed, of the averaged-out risk of being dead compared to the chance of winning the Lottery. The table gave a time after which the chances of winning the Lottery were better than those of being dead by the end of the week.

AGE	HOW LATE TO LEAVE IT
Under 16	1 hour 10 minutes
16–24	1 hour 8 minutes
5–34	51 minutes
35–44	28 minutes
45–54	11 minutes
55–64	4 minutes
65–74	1 minute
75 and over	24 seconds

It had lingered in the mind. Mr Phillips wonders what his relative chances of being dead before this week's Lottery draw are at this precise moment. In all probability they have never been better. Or worse, depending on your point of view. It would only take a single convulsive motion of one robber's finger. The feeling was the same as the one you sometimes have driving, when it occurs to you that all it would take is a strong twitch on the steering wheel and your car will go across the line into oncoming traffic, or over the kerb into a wall, or through a hedge or a ditch or a shop window, any of those things which people in film accidents do to comic or exciting effect but which in real life involve death. This is like that feeling only more so. All that would have to happen is for one of the bank robbers to conceive a dislike of Mr Phillips as he lies spreadeagled and puffing on the floor, inhaling minute particles of dog shit.

'Right, last one. Fifteen seconds,' shouts one of the men on the other side of the bank counter. Mr Phillips, if forced to guess, would say that the man is a Scouser. If the robber crosses into the bank lobby with whatever he is using to carry the money slung over his shoulder – Mr Phillips can't see, but the men are clearly jamming bank notes into some kind of bags or haversacks that they've brought with them – another item that should perhaps be banned from banks, along with crash helmets – if he comes out, points his sawn-off at Mr Phillips and blows his head off, for any reason or no reason, today, 31 July, will be the day that was lying there in wait for him all his life, hiding in the calendar, in secret parallel to 9 December, his birthday. Everybody has this day, hiding in plain sight, the one day out of the 365 which has a significance for us that we aren't here to know about. His deathday will be the day on which Mrs Phillips and the boys remember him, or remember him with particular vividness, Mrs Phillips especially. For her 31 July would be like a returning ache, every year. The boys would make a big effort to be with her, at least for the first few years, but then the practice would be less strict, it would gradually die out like a national custom that people were gradually forgetting. Only for Mrs Phillips would the day continue to have its special weight in the calendar, a day she would always dread, when she wouldn't be able to bear the sound of certain pieces of music.

Today could be the day . . . any day could be the day, of course, that is the whole point, but today especially. Mr Phillips puts his hands under his shoulders and pushes himself up. Then he gets to his feet. As he does so he realizes he is holding his hands above his shoulders, and that this gesture doesn't really make sense any more, so he lowers them. His view of what is going on in the bank is very much better from up here. In fact there's no comparison. Mr Phillips can see the way people are lying scattered in the face-down position, not radiating out from a single point but higgledy-piggledy, pointing in all directions. Clarissa Colingford, who is lying with her face turned to the right away from him, has her trousers stretched over her buttocks, not quite so stretched that the material is shiny, but nearly. It is quite a sight. He can also see the two bank robbers in the front part of the bank. Both of them are looking at him with as much of a surprised expression as it's possible to have inside a motorcycle helmet. The two men are thin and wiry. Mr Phillips probably weighs as much as one and a third of them. He says:

'I'm not doing that any more.'

'You fucking –' says one of the men, advancing towards Mr Phillips, not pointing the gun directly at him but pointing it past his side. He forgot to shout, and his accent is definitely Liverpudlian.

'Get the cunt down!' shouts the robber behind the counter who seems to be in charge. It has been at least two minutes since he shouted about its being fifteen seconds until they would finish, so perhaps something is going wrong. He does not look at Mr Phillips as he shouts but down at the counter, below which his colleague is doing something out of sight.

'I'm not going to get down,' says Mr Phillips. 'I think everyone should feel free to stand up.'

The other people in the bank are by now all looking at him, their necks doing all sorts of kinks and cricks in order to do so. People's faces are extraordinarily blank. Between them they can't notch up so much as a single expression. There is no way to tell what they are thinking. Even Clarissa Colingford, who has turned her head around and is now lying with her right cheek on the floor – she has turned around in order to get a better view of Mr Phillips! – you can see the red imprint of the carpet on her face – even Clarissa Colingford looks as she might look in a camera that was turned on her while the main camera, the one that was broadcasting live, was following someone else. Her face is off duty.

'If you don't lie down on the fucking floor you're going to get your fucking head blown off,' the nearest robber shouts – he remembers this time. His shotgun is pointed at Mr Phillips's stomach. Mr Phillips does not move.

'I think you should all get up too,' he says to the other people in the bank. 'What's the worst that can happen?'

They all stay where they are. It is what Mr Phillips would have done in their shoes. A little old lady writhes around on the floor and Mr Phillips for a moment thinks she is about to get up, but it turns out she is only manoeuvring to be more comfortable and to get a better view. The others do not make eye contact with Mr Phillips – it is psychologically and physically difficult to make eye contact with a standing man when you are lying face down on the floor – and are looking in his general direction rather than looking at him.

Mr Phillips feels a great sensation of lightness. It is as if his life is a crushing weight, a rucksack filled with bricks that he gradually got so used to he forgot it was there, and he has now managed to shift the burden so that the sense of ease, of release, is exhilarating. He feels that he could hop ten feet straight into the air. Or, more gently, just decide to float upwards, so that his perspective down on the floor-people would become steeper, and the bank robbers would crane their necks up at him in amazement, and then he would be up through the roof, looking down at the building and out across Knightsbridge, the traffic, Harrods already visible, and then further up, able to see the Victoria and Albert Museum, the way you can fly in a dream (though even in a dream you always know you're going to fall back down, and Mr Phillips has no such feeling) and then further and further up, the Thames snaking away behind and London turning into an aerial photograph and then into a map of itself, the horizon stretching further and further away, startled birds and pigeons swerving to avoid him, up through the first thin layer of wispy cloud and then further up into the clean blue, the haze of pollution and fug over the city becoming visible as it is left behind, the countryside spreading out and expanding as London shrinks, and then England shrinks, turns into an island as he gets higher and higher up, so that he can see the Channel, the crinkly coasts of Ireland and France, then the blob of Paris, so small from up here, and the Low Countries, and then Europe shrinks, and he can see out over the Atlantic, into Russia, and then the edges of the Earth itself would come into view, and Mr Phillips would float free of the planet, out into the clean nothingness of space, and suddenly the Earth would seem tiny and fragile and blue and green, shrinking fast, and most of the universe would be darkness in which the stars and planets would seem tiny, decorative, hardly disturbing the beauty and calm of the blank, lifeless void.

The bank robber nearest to Mr Phillips is looking at him

steadily and seems to be working out what to do. He half-turns to look at the other robbers and then he begins to move his shotgun upwards in the direction of Mr Phillips's head. As he does so a loud and distorted voice, coming through a megaphone, says:

'Armed police. Throw down your weapons.'

According to the very nice Detective Sergeant who took Mr Phillips's statement, the police had been acting on a tip-off. They had been following the gang for some time before the robbery and were only been waiting for them to begin the actual robbery before moving in and arresting them.

'Trouble is we were expecting three of them and a driver. When it turned out there were four of them and a driver it made things more tricky. So we decided to get them as they came out of the bank. Then you had your bright idea, sir, if you don't mind my putting it like that, and we had to come in then and there. You gave us a bit of a fright, sir.'

It was an eventful couple of minutes. When the police told the bank robbers to throw down their guns, the robber nearest Mr Phillips slowly turned round to look at his colleagues and there had been a brief moment during which the four of them had just stood and looked at one another.

'We're not getting out of here without hostages,' said the one who had seemed to be in charge. He was the first to put down his shotgun, laying it on the counter with a delicate touch – it might have been made of porcelain.

'Would they really have taken hostages?' Mr Phillips asks his policeman. They are still in the bank, where all the customers and staff who were caught up in the attempted robbery are now being interviewed to give their statements. Someone has made cups of sweet tea, saying that they are good for shock, and Mr Phillips has taken one. It is very sweet: the first cup of tea with sugar in it that he has drunk for thirty-plus years. He is being interviewed by two policemen, but the one taking the statement is doing all the talking while the other just sits there. The fact that they do things by handwriting strikes Mr Phillips as reassuring. Also the detective does not seem to be a particularly confident writer. He is concentrating hard as he scribbles away.

'It's been known,' says the policeman. 'It slightly depends on the career profile of the individual criminal. If he's got previous and he's going to go down for say ten to fifteen years anyway then he's only adding a couple of years on the end in return for maybe getting away. That's if he thinks he's a chance of getting away, and these blokes could probably tell that wasn't very likely. So no, you weren't in much danger. At least not on that count.'

'Somehow I hadn't counted on the idea of being taken hostage,' says Mr Phillips truthfully.

After the bank robbers decided not to take hostages they had all laid down their weapons and put their hands in the air, and then policemen wearing caps and bullet-proof jackets and carrying machine pistols had come into the bank, made them lie on the floor, and put handcuffs on them. Then, but not before, they said that the customers in the bank could get up.

One young man, a member of staff in a short-sleeved white shirt with pens in the top pocket that had leaked while he was lying down so that it looked as if he had been shot in the breast and bled blue blood, started laughing, a tight, breaking giggle, but no one else joined in. There had been some subdued talk – 'I thought we were for it . . . D'you think they would really have . . . Never seen anything . . .' – and then more policemen, these ones without guns and flak jackets, came in and began their interviewing. There was something dignified about the handcuffed criminals as they were led away. As the robbers were being taken out of the bank, each with at least one police-man attached to each arm, one of the little old ladies said to one of them in a tone that was shrill but still conversational – the tone you might use to speak to someone you hadn't spo-ken to for years but had collided with in the street, in which the basic hostility between you is still present in the clenched sound of your own voice – 'What do you think you're going to get out of this, then?'

For a moment it seemed as if the woman's question was going to go unanswered, but then the last of the men – not the one who had been in charge but the other one who had been behind the counter with him – said in a quiet and unexpect-edly educated voice:

'About ten years, love.'

Mr Phillips finds that it is more frightening to tell over what had happened than it had actually been living through it. He thinks: I was in a bank robbery! But the policemen are reassuringly matter of fact about the whole business, until it gets to the awkward question of what he was doing there in the first place.

'Could you confirm your place of work, sir?' the one asking the questions asks.

'Do I have to?' says Mr Phillips. The effect of this remark is to make the two policemen look at each other and then look back at him without speaking.

'I popped in to check my balance,' Mr Phillips says.

'At four thirty on a weekday,' says the hitherto silent detective.

'When your office is in the City,' says his hitherto nice colleague, in a friendly way, as if asking for clarification.

'Well, when I say it was my office, I mean it used to be my office.'

There is an interrogatory silence.

'I don't work there any more.'

'So where do you work?'

'I, er, I don't,' says Mr Phillips.

'Don't what?'

'Don't work.'

'You don't look like you don't work.' This is the nasty one again.

Mr Phillips, on the point of saying thank you, catches himself and nods instead.

'Briefcase, suit,' the nasty one adds.

'Dressed for the office, I'd say,' says the nice one.

'Yes,' says Mr Phillips.

'Yes what?'

'Yes, I'm dressed for the office.'

'But you don't work.'

'No, not any more.'

'Made redundant, were you sir?' asks the nice one.

'Yes.'

Both detectives sit back slightly.

'We see a lot of it, sir. You'd be surprised.'

'Not quite on a daily basis, I wouldn't say that, but a lot of it all the same.' This from the former Mr Nasty.

'More than you'd think.'

'It affects people in different ways.'

'Many of its effects couldn't be called small ones.'

'They're big.'

'People do things.'

'Silly things.'

'Things they wouldn't usually do.'

'They say things too.'

'Such things.'

'Sir.'

'We had one in a strangling case, didn't we, Kevin? On Hampstead Heath. Drew a map of everybody who was present. Interviewed hundreds of people. Cross referenced, little coloured pins on the map in the situation room. Reports kept turning up this chap just sitting on a bench in a three-piece suit staring into space. There all day every day. Turned out he'd been made redundant, just like you, sir. Hadn't told his family.'

'Nice chap he was too, sir.'

'Asked us not to tell his family.'

'Which we didn't.'

'Been going there for three months, hadn't he, Kevin?'

'More.'

'So you see, sir, it's nothing we haven't seen before.'

'Nothing at all.'

'We see everything all the time.'

'Think of us as being proctologists,' says the nicer of the two policemen. They share a fond smile, as at a much loved private joke.

'Is there anything else?' asks Mr Phillips when they have turned back to him.

The one with the notebook says, 'Thank you very much, sir. I'll just write this out all neat and decent, and then we'll ask you to read and sign and then you're free to go.'

'Unlike the bank robbers,' Mr Phillips says, tempted to try a joke. Neither of them reacts in any way.

Near the end of Knightsbridge Mr Phillips walks past Knightsbridge tube station, turns right and begins heading south. He
wonders if he might be on the news later in the evening. Camera crews were arriving outside the bank while the police were
doing their interviews. Someone holding a microphone had
stepped towards Mr Phillips saying 'Excuse me' as he walked
out, but Mr Phillips didn't stop and they didn't pursue him.
On the other side of the bank door, a crowd of cameramen,
women with clipboards, men with microphones and tape
recorders, and men with notebooks was standing in a circle
around Clarissa Colingford. She would certainly be in the
news, and would become even more famous. Perhaps some
other men would see her talking about her ordeal and fall in
love with her as a result. As for Mr Phillips himself, he feels
that he is over his thing about Clarissa Colingford. That was
then, this is now.

Mr Phillips plods on past the expensive shops at the top end
of Sloane Street, then down past the mansion blocks and private gardens, towards the permanent traffic jam of Sloane
Square. The rent and rates around here must be astronomical,
invisibly pushing up the prices of every frock, every watch,
every cappuccino. It occurs to Mr Phillips that what Martin

wants is to have enough money to feel at ease in places like this; to feel that, if he sees something he wants, he can simply go into a shop and buy it, without a qualm. So that places which to most people would seem to be excluding them would be open and welcoming to him, and that London would be transparent, a city of open doors.

At the pedestrian crossing in front of Mr Phillips, a girl in a Union Jack T-shirt and Doc Martens is wearing the day's second candidate for the shortest skirt he has ever seen, so short that you could see the downward bulge of her pubic mound, her cunt. Was this supposed to be the effect?

In the corner of Sloane Square, overtaking the gridlocked, honking traffic on foot, Mr Phillips passes a pub most of whose customers have spilled out on to the street. These people aren't hurrying home; not a bit of it. Many of them are office workers, mostly young. The men who wore jackets and ties to work have taken their jackets off and loosened their ties, the men who wore just T-shirts or shirts are now, most of them, bare chested, and either veal-coloured or bright pink. The women are cheerful and jaunty and eager to keep up, mainly with brightly coloured fizzy drinks but with an occasional defiant pint drinker among them. Mr Phillips was at one point – after marriage, up to the time Martin was born – a great one for stopping off after work for a couple of pints, bitter in those days, especially on Friday nights. Mrs Phillips never complained, though she might have had reason to resent the implication that he would rather spend two or three hours in the company of people he spent the whole working week with anyway, and then come home smelling of beer and smoke, when he could simply go straight home and be with her. In those days it had been as if work and pubs were mainly things men did to keep away from women. That looks different now. The women seem just as noisy, just as confident, and just as keen on having a good time. It is hard to tell what they are getting away from.

The truth is, Mr Phillips feels that he could murder a pint of lager. And why not? He sidesteps his way through the energetically boozing, laughing, flirting, gossiping loose scrum outside the pub and pushes into the dark interior. Here there is a wall of cigarette smoke, loud Martin-type pop music, fruit machines twinkling brightly in the half-gloom, and fewer people than there are out on the pavement. The drinkers outside in the street seem recreational; those inside are more businesslike. At the bar, a group of men who have made an early start and are already quite drunk are arguing over an article about football in the *Evening Standard*.

'He'd never fucking have. He just wouldn't,' says a man in a yellow sweatshirt leaning back against the bar with his elbows on the counter – an oddly upper-class pose.

'It says here he fucking was,' says the man brandishing the newspaper.

'He's capable of fucking anything,' grumbles a third into the glass he was raising to his mouth. 'The cunt.'

'Well as far as I'm concerned he can fuck off,' says the first man.

'Now you've said something I agree with,' says the paper-brandishing man to general agreement.

The two bar staff are keeping well out of range of this, at the other end of the counter. Mr Phillips tries leaning over the bar, the edge jabbing into the uppermost part of his stomach in a not unpleasant way, and smiling in their general direction. It does not work.

'Excuse me,' he finally calls out, the demand sounding more like an apology than he means it to. One of the barmen looks over at him and with visible reluctance breaks off his conversation to come and attend to Mr Phillips. He is wearing what is supposed to be a uniform of white short-sleeved shirt and black trousers, but is doing so with an unbuttoned dishevelment that is clearly meant to be insubordinate. When he gets opposite Mr Phillips he simply raises his eyebrows. He is chewing gum.

'Pint of lager,' says Mr Phillips, consciously and effortfully repressing the impulse to say 'please'. The youth takes a glass up from beneath the counter, holds it under the brightly neon-decorated handle and flicks the beer pump on with his spare hand. The urban day is full of moments like these, when conversation and social exchange would be natural, but don't happen, because of the weight of the city pressing down on every interaction. If you started talking to strangers, where would it stop? Somewhere in his heart Mr Phillips has a fantasy of a country life that is different, where the shopkeeper bored you rigid for ten minutes on the subject of how he had been swindled out of third prize for his competition turnips at the county show when you popped in to get a pint of semi-skimmed milk, and where every visit to the pub was a long, warm bath-like soak in collective and individual grievances against outsiders, landowners, the council, the government, the European Union, in short anyone not present; a life where you nodded at and chatted to everyone you bumped into – except people with whom you were in mid-feud – as a matter of course. And perhaps that life or a version of it is now possible, if they cash in the £100,000 of the redeemed part of their mortgage and buy a place in the country. Not the south-east – for that kind of money it would have to be somewhere pretty but cheap; say Herefordshire, a little stone town house or an old post office or a comfy new bungalow. Mrs Phillips could tout for music lessons – it wouldn't be that difficult, people would be looking for things to do – Thomas would go to the local school for what would after all only be one more year, Mr Phillips would set himself up as a posh London chartered accountant doing a favour for the rustics. He wouldn't put it quite like that but that would be the gist. The country must be full of clueless self-employed people in need of help with their sums. Everything is possible.

'Two pounds fifteen,' says the bartender, spilling some lager as he puts the astonishingly expensive pint down on a little rubber mat in front of Mr Phillips. Raising his eyebrows to register a dignified protest, Mr Phillips reaches for his wallet and as he does so realizes that he has forgotten to check his balance, the whole official reason for his expedition into the bank in the first place. Keeping his five pound note for dealings with politer tradesmen, he hands over a twenty. It's a badly crumpled note, a reminder, among other things, of how amazingly resilient is the paper used in making money.

'Got anything smaller?' sneers the young man.

Not for nothing a born Londoner, Mr Phillips has his own reserves of rudeness. Looking straight and expressionlessly at the bartender he very slowly shakes his head. (This despite the bus change which is still heavy in his trouser pocket. But there comes a time when you have to make a stand.) The bartender goes off and does noisy things at the electronic till, coming back with a ten pound note and a large fistful of coins.

'No fives,' says the youth, holding out a fistful of coins palm downwards and decanting them into the upturned cup of Mr Phillips's hands. Mr Phillips forwards the small avalanche of metal into his pocket. He takes his drink out from the depressing interior of the pub past the sign saying No Drinking On The Pavement into the happy throng of people drinking on the pavement. He finds a small patch of wall with a ledge and puts his drink on it, and then puts down his briefcase to mark his territory. A few feet away, an after-office group are roaring at one of their colleagues who is doing an impersonation of a man performing Chinese martial arts exercises in slow motion. He is standing on one foot with both arms above his head, puffing out his mouth and making a high-pitched mewing sound.

As he comes out of his Tube train at Embankment, Mr Phillips can feel the pint of beer being shaken up inside him along with everything else he has eaten that day to make a giant cocktail of lager and porridge and bacon and scallops and G and T and coffee and banana and fish cake. Presumably the contents of your stomach look like what comes out of you when you are sick. That thought, the bubbles in the lager and the jolting action of the train help Mr Phillips to feel mildly but definitely nauseated. Mr Phillips lets the flow of commuters sweep him up the escalator, on to the concourse. He comes out of the station, out across the place in front where taxis and passengers mingle, and heads down the alley at the side towards the footbridge over the Thames. There are always a good few beggars about and today is no exception.

The pedestrian bridge is one of Mr Phillips's favourites. He likes its narrowness and air of fragility, the way it makes him feel as if he is hanging in the air above the river.

This is the next-to-last leg of his journey home, and in an ideal world Mr Phillips would stop for a look at the river, but with single files of people hurrying over the narrow bridge in both directions it isn't really possible, so he passes on at a slightly too quick walk and arrives breathless on the South

Bank. As always it looks like an unlovely concrete animal sprawled out in death. He crosses the walkway, past an immensely unflattering bust of Nelson Mandela, and heads towards the train station. This is as close as he usually gets to the National Theatre; in fact, Mr Phillips has only ever been in the building once, to go and see *King Lear* when Martin was studying it for A-level. Mrs Phillips set the trip up and then disloyally but genuinely came down with flu that same morning. Mr Phillips, with a sense that he was behaving very well, volunteered to go instead. In retrospect he sees it as one of the longest four hours of his life, uncannily similar, in the sensation of discomfort, anxiety and pure duration, to that of waiting in Casualty.

'What did you think?' he risked asking Martin afterwards, on the way back to the car park. This was a scruffy patch of nothing land which by itself proved that you were now in South London, since car parks in North London were all claustrophobically underground or elaborately above, with ramps and lifts and one-way signs. The two Phillipses had agreed to award themselves a McDonalds on the way home.

'It was long,' said Martin. 'It's always long.'

'I felt sorry for the man who had to take all his clothes off,' said Mr Phillips.

'Edgar,' said Martin. 'Small cock, too.'

Mr Phillips emerges from the overground tunnel into the main station concourse at Waterloo. One of the nice things about the

226

way it's all changed in the last couple of decades is the sudden arrival here of dinky shops, where you can buy not just a newspaper, as you always could, but flowers and chocolates and compact discs, and there is also a whole shop devoted to interesting socks, and another to cappuccino, and now you can even go downstairs on an impulse and get on a train to Paris or Brussels, just like that. In three and a bit hours he could be in a café on the left bank of the Seine wearing a beret, making gnoghi gnoghi noises and eating horsemeat and chips. Or he could be in Brussels eating whatever it was Belgians ate. He could learn the language, get a job as an accountant specializing in multilingual transactions, companies that sold lingerie to the British or spark plugs to the French or whatever. The system couldn't be that different, the whole point about double entry bookkeeping was that it was the same wherever you went. He would do well over there, they would like his style and be charmed by Mrs Phillips – so unpretentious – so natural – and she plays like an angel! He would have an apartment in the middle of Paris, because the French tended to live in flats, and a little house in the country, Normandy perhaps, with a neighbour who kept an eye on things and whom he paid biannually in his famous home-made cider. Or alternatively he could become a tramp, only a French tramp, cadging francs for Gauloises and rough wine. Probably he would gravitate southwards where the weather was better. He could buy a packet of chalk and do drawings on the pavement. He could have a little French dog for company. If he went and got out the maximum on his credit card now, and then drew the maximum from his bank account, and bought a ticket for Paris, and tried to disappear, how far would I get, Mr Phillips wonders? How determined did you have to be if you wanted your life never to catch up with you?

There is something comforting about the huge board of departures above the main platform concourse. Not just Clapham Junction but Wimbledon, Sutton, Godalming, Putney Heath, Southfields, Queenstown Road, Southampton, Portsmouth. All these places which to somebody are a synonym for Home. Waterloo in the morning is an anxious place, full of the late-for-work, whereas at the end of the day, though it is just as full of people who are hurrying just as hard, for Mr Phillips it seems obscurely comfy.

There is a Clapham Junction train from platform four, ultimate destination Portsmouth, at three minutes past six, and another four minutes after that. The platform will close thirty seconds before departure because that way more people miss the train. Mr Phillips none the less decides to take a chance on trying to catch the 6.03 and breaks into a portly, shuffling half-jog. He must have taken more exercise today than in the whole of the previous year. Others of a similar mind are making a similar last-minute dash, and Mr Phillips is overtaken by a woman in a short tan skirt and a man wearing, for some reason, a raincoat of the same colour. They are giggling and holding hands, as they run down the platform and hop on the second carriage. Good luck to them. In Mr Phillips's experience so many people avoid the nearest carriage on the assumption that it will be the most full, and instead get into the next carriage along, or even the next but one, that it is often those carriages which are the fullest whereas the nearest carriage is in fact, relatively speaking, reasonably empty. As you get older you make up in cunning for what you lose in speed.

Mr Phillips gets into the first carriage and takes the penultimate available seat, choosing the space beside a plump, affluent-looking man in a business suit in preference to the space beside a girl who is chewing gum and looking either out of the window or at her own reflection. She looks like an eighteen year old who looks like a fifteen year old, with off-blonde hair, puppy-fat cheeks and a full, slightly sulky mouth: a dirty old man's type of girl. Mr Phillips wants to sit beside her but senses that his reasons for doing so would be too transparent; plus, he is worried about being smelly. Plus the seat he opted for has a discarded copy of the *Evening Standard* on it.

Two paces behind him a thirty to fortyish man who looks like he works in the City comes in behind Mr Phillips and takes the seat beside the girl. He doesn't seem to notice her. He is carrying a briefcase and a carrier bag, which he opens to produce a bottle of wine wrapped in tissue paper. He gingerly takes the paper off the wine and, holding the bottle up on his knees, begins reading, or at least looking at, the label, in an apparent trance of reverent concentration.

With gratifying punctuality, the train doors squeal an alarm and then wheeze shut. There is a jolt and they begin to move out from underneath the train shed, past the spaghetti tangle of tracks outside the station, where there is a sudden expansion of the view out over South London, mainly low buildings with the occasional ugly office complex or disastrous sixties tower block. On working days this was just about Mr Phillips's favourite moment in the whole twenty-four hours: the last leg of his trip home. Even as a boy his favourite journey had been the trip home, and his best moment in any excursion the point at which the outward leg of the expedition was over and they turned back to base. That feels less true today. He can't claim to be particularly looking forward to getting home and the prospect of an evening in front of the telly doing more or less nothing.

Mr Phillips scans the *Evening Standard* quickly as the train bangs along. For him the etiquette of picking up a paper on a train is that you can read it on the train or other public place but you then have to leave it behind in your turn. Otherwise it is as if you have stolen it. So he doesn't have long. Most of the news is the usual. On page seven however there is a story about a pair of mime artists who were taking part in the festival of street theatre that is going on in London for the next three days until they were arrested for outraging public decency. They had dressed up as a tramp and a schoolgirl and pretended to have sex together on an Underground train. Their mistake was to pick a carriage with an off-duty policeman in it. The crime carries a maximum sentence of twelve months.

The train roars through Vauxhall station without stopping and then a few minutes later begins to slow down as it approaches Clapham Junction. Various people begin to make This Is My Stop preparations. The man with the wine bottle starts gently wrapping the tissue paper back around his treasure. The girl beside him stops looking at her reflection and adjusts a plastic folder she is holding to her chest. With sadness Mr Phillips sees that the folder is a brochure from a modelling agency called Model Models. It is as if no pretty girl can just be a pretty girl any more, it has to be a job or an ambition.

Mr Phillips squeezes up and out of his seat and stands gripping the rail beside the compartment door. The metal has the slick coolness of an object that has been touched by many hands since it was last cleaned, and it is hard to suppress thoughts about flu germs, tropical viruses, people who don't wash their hands after wiping their arses. Mr Phillips is not phobic or hypersensitive about these things but sometimes they cross his mind. The train stops, the doors make their noises and open, and Mr Phillips hops across the gap on to the platform.

Mr Phillips comes out on to the bleak rear entrance of the station, where he faces a few disconsolate and halfhearted tower blocks, many of them ex-council flats now sold into private ownership. There is also a depressed-looking dentist's and a meeting house for Seventh Day Adventists, both of them made out of concrete and appearing as if they were designed to be used as places of defensive entrenchment in the event of war or major civil unrest.

Weaving in between these low buildings, Mr Phillips wonders if the bank robbery will have already been on the news when he gets home, or whether that sort of thing makes the news at all. On the three or four times he has passed what looked like horrific traffic accidents – once when policemen seemed to be shampooing, or at least hosing down, blood off the Cromwell Road after an accident between, of course, a white van and a motorbike – he always expected to be hearing about it in gory detail when he sat down with the telly, but never yet had, not once. These things must be too common-place to be reported. Perhaps bank robberies and stick-ups were like that also, going on all the time as part of the normal background life of the city.

At the point where Mr Phillips emerges on to Kestrel Lane for the last five minutes of the walk home, he nearly bumps into an old woman who is carrying three or four plastic bags and is stooped over like a question mark from the effort. She is moving so slowly that she has turned herself into an obstacle. Mr Phillips swerves past her and heads onward, glad to have avoided a collision that would only have ended in his making apologies he didn't believe. (Sorry, Mr Phillips will say, when someone treads on his foot.)

Mr Phillips doesn't think much about what it would be like to be old, since he can't imagine living longer than his father, who died at the age of sixty-one. Not that he thinks he is going to pop his clogs at any moment; but he just can't picture it other than to entertain very vague mental images of himself at eighty dandling great-grandchildren, or effortfully blowing out a single tiny candle at his crowded ninetieth. He can however imagine that things just get worse and worse, and that the difficulties he has accumulated with his own body, the fatness and sweatiness and occasional out-of-breathness, his stiff morning back and pee-again prostate, his sour and reluctant-to-settle stomach acid, the sense that the face in the mirror was an unwelcome growth attached to his real face (which is thirty years younger); all these things would just get worse, so that he would be hugely fat, wheezing, barely able to walk, stooped, racked by arthritic pains, constantly peeing, chronically dyspeptic, ugly and malodorous, with in addition all the unexpected nastiness that would suddenly crop up, new diseases, a dodgy liver, dizzy spells, impetigo, insomnia, asthma, diverticulitis, any nasty surprise, basically, except Aids (chance would be a fine thing). All that is in store. The little old lady whom Mr Phillips has just overtaken looks as if she lives in a country where all these things are just part of an ordinary day.

Mr Phillips turns around and goes back towards her. In the time he has taken to go a hundred yards she has moved about twenty feet. As he walks up to the bent and wrapped figure he sees that she is alarmed by his approach. Frightened of me! Imagine!

'Excuse me,' says Mr Phillips, 'can I help?'

She stops to listen. The woman's expression says very clearly that the effort of stopping and starting and thinking the

233

proposition over is not welcome. At the same time there is a shrewdness there, too. She is sizing up the likelihood that he will seize her bags and do a runner. She has, though, a nice face, a tiny bit whiskery but bright-eyed and open.

'Can I help with your bags?' Mr Phillips says.

She takes a moment to think this over and then without saying anything puts her bags down on the pavement, all four of them, though not her handbag, which she keeps over the crook of her arm. She has an unexpectedly good bending technique, flexing her knees rather than bending her back.

'Thank you,' says the woman, after she has put her bags down.

'Are we going far?'

'Over there,' she says, pointing at the tower blocks that had once belonged to the council and now are a mix of public and private housing. Most of the new tenants are people like Martin, yuppies. This woman is one of the older generation of council tenants, the aboriginal inhabitants of this part of town, gradually being driven out by the influx of money.

'Fine,' says Mr Phillips. He picks up the bags, two in each hand, which with his briefcase makes five in all. The bags come from Asda, about ten minutes' walk away for Mr Phillips and who knew how long for her. They are not light. She must wait for her pension and do all the week's shopping in one go. Mr Phillips suspects that if he were in a similar position he would be inclined to do his shopping on a daily basis, popping out for a tin of baked beans and a loaf of bread one day, a pair of lamb chops and a baking potato the next – a daily trip or expedition.

'I was getting a bit short of puff,' the old woman says in a more confiding and cheery way.

'It's a big shop you've done,' says Mr Phillips. She gives a small titter.

'Monday is my day for them.'

'My wife does all our shopping.'

'You're lucky.'

Am I? thinks Mr Phillips. They arrive at the barred gate to the block of flats. There is a little metal keypad where the old lady types in a four-digit entry code: 2146, Mr Phillips can't help but notice. If people in the towers do the Lottery quite a few of them will probably use that same code, so if it ever comes up in the winning sequence there could be a mysterious rash of instant millionaires in the flats. The lift shafts would ring to the popping of champagne corks, the forecourts would suddenly become clogged with Bentley convertibles. The latch buzzes and the gate clicks open, the woman helping it swing wider by leaning on it with her shoulder. Mr Phillips squeezes through after her.

'Nearly there,' she says. She can clearly see that he is struggling. Mr Phillips can feel his breath becoming short and chesty. They cross a concrete garden where someone's determined efforts to brighten things up with flower beds and paint have created an enhanced air of desolation. A hose that has been left trained into a flower bed is leaking into a big brown

235

puddle of floating dirt. I'm glad I don't live here, thinks Mr Phillips. I'm glad I'm not old. Somewhere just out of sight children's voices are being sharply raised in either anger or play.

The doors to the ground floor of the flats are opaque glass reinforced by squares of metal thread. On one wall is an array of mailboxes, a handsome piece of wooden furniture that is obviously too small for modern amounts of junk mail and leaflets, since many of the pigeonholes are visibly stuffed to the brim, like ballot boxes in a rigged election, and there is a surf of leaflets and take-away menus on the floor beneath. On the wall beside that is a dark stairwell and a not very salubrious looking lift. The entrance hall is illuminated by a fluorescent light that makes Mr Phillips feel he might be on the point of fainting or having a fit until he realizes the flickering has to do with it and not him.

The old woman presses the button and the lift doors open immediately. Lifts, like tunnels, are not Mr Phillips's strong point, except for the nice modern ones with glass that you can see out of. This one is not like that: it is a shiny metal box, long and narrower at the ends than in the middle – a coffin shape. Of course coffins would be one of the things it is used for, as the older residents died out and their children or grandchildren sold their flats. Despite the fact that everyone who lived there was getting inexorably older, the average age of the inhabitants would gradually go down – an apparent defiance of the laws of physics.

However much he dislikes the look of the lift there is now no question of being able to avoid travelling in it, so Mr Phillips gets in, with feelings of trepidation. The first thing he does whenever he enters a lift is to check that there is an escape hatch overhead – not that he has any notions about clambering up there, but it is reassuring to know that you can open a hatch to get some more oxygen if the lift breaks down. The next thing he checks is the emergency alarm or (better) speaker or (best) phone. But this lift has nothing but a seamless metal roof and although it does have a phone the phone has an Out of Order sign attached to it. It is the worst lift in the world.

The little old lady presses the button to the fourteenth floor. The button lights up, the lift doors bang together, and after a tiny but horrible dip downwards the lift lurches and begins to go up. Covertly inspecting the overhead display Mr Phillips can see that the fourteenth floor is actually the thirteenth, and that the number has been changed as a concession to superstition. This is something that he has never been able to work out. If you thought there was something dangerous about the number thirteen, surely the thirteenth floor would be dangerous whatever you called it, since it is the fact of thirteen and not the word that is the problem? It was treating the gods or the fates or God himself – not that this was the sort of thing you would expect Him to bother about – as if He was very stupid to think that they or He wouldn't notice.

The lift, which has rocked and banged all the way up, stops at the so-called fourteenth floor. There is a terrible moment of absolute stillness and then the doors creak slowly open. The woman, taking charge, moves into the hallway outside, which has been painted in peeling grey-green and is lit by another flickering fluorescent strip-light. She turns left along the narrow corridor, walks past two doors, through one of which Mr Phillips can hear loud pop music being played on a low-fidelity radio. The third door along the corridor is hers. It has a brass knocker as well as a bell, a metal plate carrying the number 46 made out of the same brass, and an extra lock. She has already taken her key out of the bag as she arrives at the door, and she manipulates the locks in sequence with the ease of much practice. It is a thing people do in cities now, Mr Phillips knew, he had seen an item about it on *Crimewatch*. They get their keys ready in advance. That way you are less likely to have someone come up behind you and bop you on the head.

But the inside of the flat is a surprise. When he comes through the door behind the woman he finds that he is looking across the room to a huge picture window, through which the blue evening sky looks like an abstract painting. At one end, occupying the whole wall, is a waist-height bookshelf, very tidy, with dozens of framed photographs resting on it. Many of them feature younger versions of this woman with a big man of about the same age. She is a pretty little thing in the early photos. The man is a bruiser, somehow familiar-looking, with lots of black then lots of white hair. He is a good bit taller than her, and is usually wearing a tie.

Copying the woman's good lifting technique, Mr Phillips

bends at the knees and sets the bags and his briefcase down. The plastic handles have dug deeply into his hands and left livid red, white and purple marks that look as if they will never fade. Glancing around the room, Mr Phillips sees what is right beside him: a fish tank, the length of the whole side wall, full of the most highly coloured fish he could ever imagine. The tank is decorated with grey rocks and green moss and the fish look as bright as jewels. There is a small shoal of tiny black ones with red go-faster stripes, darting and flitting around the tank, and one big electric-blue fish floating motionless apart from a slow opening and closing of its mouth. Some other indeterminate-sized fish float and glint, and one, green and blue with a cheeky expression, hovers beside an updraught of bubbles in the middle of the tank, looking for all the world like a man undertaking a decadent pleasure such as sucking on a hookah.

'Amazing fish,' says Mr Phillips.

'They were my husband's,' says the woman, from the kitchen, where she has gone with two of the bags that Mr Phillips set down. A few seconds later she comes back carrying a large box of fish food, which she carries over to the tank.

'I wondered what was so heavy in there,' says Mr Phillips.

'You'd be surprised how much they get through.' And then, as she begins tipping the food into the tank, moving from side to side to give all the fish a fair whack, and the fish start to feed, she adds, 'I'm Martha.'

'I'm Victor. Pleased to meet you,' says Mr Phillips.

'They were his passion,' she says, nodding at the fish tank.

'They're quite something.'

'He would have preferred dogs, but it's not fair to them, is it? With the space.'

'No.'

'Not that those are all the same, his actual fish. They don't live for ever.'

'What's this one?' asked Mr Phillips, pointing at the motionless whopper in the middle of the tank.

'That's Boris. He's a parrot fish. Brian named him after a man he knew.'

'He's very handsome.'

'He eats more than all the others put together.'

Mr Phillips has heard that goldfish, if they escaped into the wild, would grow to an unlimited size. But there seems to be no tactful way of asking about this.

'They liven up the flat,' says the woman on a concluding note. She picks up the other two bags and takes them into the kitchen, from where she calls out, 'Would you like a cup of tea?'

'I'd better not,' says Mr Phillips.

'I'll be making one for myself anyway,' says Martha.

'Well, that's very nice of you,' says Mr Phillips.

'Make yourself at home. I'll only be a minute,' she says. At some point, while he was not looking, she has managed to take off her coat.

Mr Phillips goes across to the window. It is an amazing view; you can suddenly see why people want to live in these flats. He is looking north-eastwards across the middle of London, and can see the Post Office Tower, the Houses of Parliament and St Paul's, all three. A residue of his Catholic education is that high places always make him think of the Devil tempting Jesus in the wilderness, taking him up high into the air and offering him the world. In this light it looks like a pretty good deal. His own house, about five minutes' walk away, is not visible from here: a small block of offices cuts off the line of sight. But he can see the railway line that eventually runs behind the houses across his road, and the single green field, grandly called Wilmington Park, where people take their dogs to crap.

Martha comes back carrying a tray which has a teapot underneath a bulbous cosy, cups and saucers, a bowl of sugar cubes and a plate of biscuits. She puts the tray down on a low table beside a reclining armchair that faces a small, old television. A touch of bustle about her movements makes Mr Phillips see she is enjoying having company.

'Sugar?'

'White without, please.'

Mr Phillips tastes his tea.

'Best drink of the day,' says Martha, who then blushes. 'Brian used always to say that.'

'What did your husband do?' asks Mr Phillips. There are no photographs of children so he does not feel that is a safe question.

'He was a teacher,' says Martha. 'RE. At St Aloysius's, for over thirty years.'

'I was at St Aloysius's,' says Mr Phillips. 'What was his surname?'

'Erith.'

'Mr Erith! He taught me! I remember him! I thought I recognized his picture! He was very . . .'

Mr Phillips runs into trouble at this point. Mr Erith was the loony RE teacher who talked about St Augustine and sin all the time. 'Mad' was the word that would honestly come next.

'. . . he was a very good teacher,' Mr Phillips finishes.

He gets up and goes across to the photographs. Sure enough, that is Mr Erith, looking more relaxed and casual than he had done at school, but the same man none the less. And now Mr Phillips notices the titles of the books. *Gravity and Grace. Church Dogmatics. Mere Christianity. The Screwtape Letters. The Sickness Unto Death. Either/Or. The Varieties of Religious Experience.* Mr Erith.

'He . . . I never knew he kept fish.'

'Tropical fish.'

'He was a very memorable teacher,' says Mr Phillips. 'I often think of him still.'

Martha, with great dignity, simply smiles. Then she reaches down under her chair and takes out a thick album which she shyly opens and hands across to Mr Phillips. For a second he thinks it is more photographs, but then he sees that it is a series of embroidered mottoes, obviously something Martha has made herself. The first of them, in pink against a purple background decorated with flowers, says: 'The masses need something that will give them a thrill of power. A new age of magical interpretation of the world is at hand, of interpretation in terms of the will and not of the intelligence'. Below that, in smaller lettering but the same shade of pink, it says, 'Adolph Hitler'.

'I say,' says Mr Phillips.

'He kept a little notebook of sayings he liked,' says Martha. 'I started doing this after he died as . . .'

Mr Phillips decides she means as something to do, or as a way of remembering him. There are several more embroidered pages in the album. The next one says: 'Happiness is the maximum agreement of reality and desire. Joseph Stalin'. It is yellow on a blue background with an abstract pattern. The one after that says: 'The waste even in a fortunate life, the isolation even of a life rich in intimacy, cannot but be felt deeply, and is the central feeling of tragedy. William Empson.' That one is all in different shades of green. 'Nothing, whether deed, word, thought, or text, ever happens in relation, positive or negative, to anything that precedes, follows or exists elsewhere, but only as a random act whose power, like the power of death, is due to the randomness of its occurrence. Paul de Man.'

'Golly,' says Mr Phillips. He closes the book.

'Do you mind my asking something?' he says. 'The boys at school always used to speculate about what Mr Erith had done before he became a teacher. I don't know why, quite. He just didn't seem the teacher type.'

'I got so many letters when Brian died. Quite a few of his old pupils said that. Some of them still write.'

243

'How, er, how long?'

'Five years,' says Martha. 'Sometimes it seems like twenty years, and sometimes like ten minutes.'

'Yes, it's like that, isn't it?'

Martha seems to be remembering things. There is silence for a while, and then she says:

'He trained to be a priest. He was in the seminary for two years as a young man, and then he left. He started to disagree with all sorts of specific points of doctrine. The main thing was that he became convinced that God didn't create the world. He said that nothing about the world made sense if you thought it was made by God whereas if you thought it was made by the Devil, a lot of things were much more clear. Your duty was to leave it behind and get closer to God. So you were supposed to reject this world in favour of a higher one. But he kept all that to himself in later life.' She smiles again. 'Did he used to talk about sin a lot?'

'He did, rather.'

'He always did that. He used to say it was the only bit of religion schoolboys had any interest in.'

'I hope you don't mind me saying so, but we thought he was a bit bonkers.'

Martha makes a face.

'He knew that most of the boys thought that. He said it was a good way of getting them to listen.'

'I didn't realize he lived here. I'd have come to see him.' Even as he says it Mr Phillips wonders if it is true. He and Martha drink their tea.

Back down on the street, his knees trembling and stinging from the thirteen-storey descent down the dank stairwell, Mr Phillips set out on the last stretch home. He weaves down Kestrel Lane, past the Afro-Caribbean barber and the travel shop and the two small supermarkets, and then crosses into the residential quiet of Middleton Way. The cutting-through cars have disappeared for the evening. On the pavement in front of him, at what can only be a highly uncomfortable angle, are a pair of legs. They belong to a man who is lying on his back underneath a battered blue Ford Fiesta. Beside the legs are an open toolbox, a can of WD40 and an oily rag. This is no surprise to Mr Phillips, since this near-neighbour is very often to be found in exactly this position, especially at evenings and weekends. Leaving his toolbox there where anyone could steal it while he lies trapped under the car seems a trusting gesture, like a well-adjusted dog lying on its back to sleep.

Rounding the corner from Middleton Way, Mr Phillips is nearly run over by a boy on roller-skates, dressed from head to toe in shiny cycling clothes – Lycra shorts, orange top, blue helmet. 'Sorry,' the boy calls out over his shoulder as he vooms past. Mr Phillips doesn't recognize him.

And then Mr Phillips turns into Wellesley Crescent. Most

people have already got home and there is hardly anywhere left to park. Happily there is no sign of Mr Palmer, a.k.a. Norman the Noxious Neighbour. Mr and Mrs Wu from the Neighbourhood Watch meeting are standing on their doorstep, chatting to a man in overalls whom Mr Phillips hasn't seen before. On the other side of the street, though, outside Mr Phillips's house, is a much more surprising sight. Thomas is standing with his shirt off beside a bucket of soapy water, carrying a sponge which he dumps on top of Mr Phillips's car windscreen, squeezes, and then wipes across the glass. Thomas, in short, is washing the car. This is such an unexpected vision that Mr Phillips stops short. But he doesn't want Thomas to see him standing there just watching, so he gets moving again and comes up behind his son, who turns just as he arrives at the now gleaming Honda.

'Thomas!' says Mr Phillips. 'You're washing the car.'

Thomas laughs and resumes his dunk-squeeze-wipe gesture over the windshield, whose wipers are folded back and pointed into the air like insect antennae.

'Felt like it,' says Thomas. 'You're late. Mum was starting to get worried,' he added.

'Forgot something,' says Mr Phillips. He thinks about asking if Tom will be in this evening but decides against it on the grounds that his son might think he is pushing his luck. And the car really does look very clean.

'I'll, er, I'll see you later,' says Mr Phillips. 'That's really nice of you about the car.'

'That's OK.'

Mr Phillips pushes the front door but it is off the latch. He replaces a dustbin lid which has been blown or knocked off and fumbles for his keys, which he finds in his left-hand jacket pocket, and opens the door. He has no idea what will happen next.